Betting on Brian

A Sweet Contemporary Aladdin Retelling

Becki Lee

Literary Escapes Press

Betting on Brian, First Printing: June 2024

Literary Escapes Press

Edited by Rachel Shipp Editing

Paperback ISBN: 978-1-960969-13-2

eBook ISBN: 978-1-960969-12-5

Contents

To mom and dad
for all the fairy tales you read to me as a child
I wish you were here to read this one

Prologue

MICHAEL

THE MOON HUNG LOW in the Nashville sky cast an ominous glow over a figure moving through the corridors of the state capitol. Senator Michael Black—a man of cultivated charm, good looks, and barely concealed malevolence—stood at the precipice of his most audacious plan yet, one he'd been working toward for most of his life.

He entered his dark office and pulled the chain on a desk lamp, sending long shadows around the room. He didn't waste space on his large mahogany desk with family pictures or knickknacks; it was merely a place to bring his plans to fruition. He sat in the black leather chair—he liked to think of it as his throne—pleased with the way the day had progressed.

His bill, the Digital Well-Being and Algorithmic Transparency Act, had passed. Just barely, but it passed. Robert St. Claire, of St. Claire Industries and Technologies, would be pleased. And not only would St. Claire be pleased, he was now indebted to Michael. At the moment, that was all that mattered. St. Claire was one of his biggest contributors, and it paid, literally, to keep him happy.

Michael picked up his cell phone to make the call—this didn't need to go through the capitol switchboard. He paced in front of a window overlooking the lights of Nashville and stared at the reflection cast by the soft light of the lamp. The dim lighting made him look harsh. His stubbled cheeks seemed hollow and angular, his dark eyes stared back with an almost sinister glow.

If my constituents could see me now, he thought with a jaded laugh. At fifty-five, he worked hard to present well on the campaign trail and in front of his colleagues. His "hard luck, bootstrap" story resonated with his base, and they'd kept him in office for ten years.

But it was only half of who he was. His other half...well, he kept it out of the public eye. That part of him was set on vengeance. An eye for an eye.

It had been easy to work hard through the years, his goal of revenge always in mind. He voted on bills he knew were important to his people and his party. Worked his way up in seniority. And finally found his way to the Future Technology and Innovation Committee.

Now his end goal was in sight.

"Yes?" A man answered.

"It's done," Black said simply.

"The bill passed?"

"It did." He paused to let the news sink in. "I've kept up my end of the deal..." He left the sentence hanging.

The man on the other end of the line sighed heavily. "Yes. You have."

A small smile flitted across Black's thin lips. "I'll see you at the gala in a couple of weeks. We'll talk there."

He disconnected the call. He'd won. This moment had taken twenty long years of hard work, but it was all worth it.

The St. Claire family would pay.

Chapter 1

KRISI

Nashville Princess Back Home

After years abroad, local socialite Kristine St. Claire has returned to Nashville. Sources say she is tucked away in the family palace, the St. Claire mansion. Of course the sudden demise of her relationship with racecar driver Jacque Barro may have something to do with her return.

St. Claire and Barro had been an item on the Paris social scene for four months. Sparks flew the moment they met at an event at Versailles, and their relationship has been filled with fireworks, though continual rumors of his infidelity circled around.

One could imagine the pictures of Barro and a young—very young—model in compromising positions, didn't help their relationship. Kristine spent a few weeks licking her wounded heart in her Paris apartment before returning to her hometown, looking lovelier than ever.

Sunlight spilled into Krisi St. Claire's bedroom as the silk curtains were yanked open. Her pale pink silk eye mask might have saved her from the onslaught of light, but it couldn't save her from the efficient personal assistant.

"Rise and shine, princess," Nikki said in a singsong voice as she straightened the drapes.

Krisi ignored her and cocooned deeper into her soft, warm fortress.

"Sorry, darlin', but it's Monday. You have a busy day. You need to get your pampered rear end out of that ridiculous bed."

Krisi opened her eyes and pushed up the eye mask to see Nikki shaking her head at the four-poster extravaganza.

Krisi let out a deep sigh. "Okay, okay." She held up her finger to say *one moment*. "Three wishes first." She closed her eyes again, and her hand went to the gold chain around her neck. Her fingers slid to the small gold genie's lamp and rubbed it gently.

- *Strong coffee.*

- *A beautiful day.*

- *New friendship.*

Nikki stayed quiet through the morning ritual, then grinned when Krisi opened her eyes and threw off the embroidered teal coverlet and sent several pillows tumbling to the floor. Krisi swung her legs over the side of the bed and sat up.

"And," Krisi said as her feet hit the plush rug next to her bed, "you're not wrong about this bed. It *is* ridiculous. I can't imagine what my parents were thinking when they redecorated my bedroom. It certainly wasn't me."

Nikki shook her head and joined Krisi in looking around the room that had been their childhood sanctuary. The once soothing palette had been updated to resemble a garish boudoir, adorned with heavy, ornate furniture, lights dripping with crystals, pale gold silk wall fabric, and deep jewel tones on the bedspread and pillows.

Krisi stretched her arms over her head, enjoying the feel of silky pajamas sliding over her torso before she turned to Nikki. "What's so almighty important you felt the need to wake me at the crack of dawn?"

Nikki rolled her eyes. Having grown up with Krisi, almost as sisters, she knew her moods. "You always turn into a diva when we come to your parents' house. It's already eight o'clock, hardly the crack of dawn. Besides, it's a beautiful May day, and you have a coffee date with Grace Montgomery. I know you're probably jet-lagged, but you asked me to wake you up."

Jet lag seemed to affect her a little more each year. At thirty-two, it took her a few days to adjust to the time difference. But just the mention of the impending coffee date perked Krisi up. She'd been looking forward to this meeting for months. Life in Paris had become unbearable, and she hoped her return to Nashville would move her out of the limelight and into a life more grounded.

Which is where Grace came in. She ran a women's shelter in the mountains outside Nashville. Actually, Grace had bought Krisi's cabin and converted it into the shelter. And now Krisi was on the team to raise funds for the shelter.

She knew she lived a privileged life. As an heir to the St. Claire billions, her childhood had been...different. Nikki's mom was her nanny and had probably saved Krisi from becoming an out-of-control diva. Having Nikki as her best friend and personal assistant kept her grounded now.

They'd lived in Europe for the last several years, with Paris as their last stop. Meeting Grace nearly a year and a half ago lit a spark inside her, and it had been simmering since. She'd woken up to wanting *more*. Not just from life and relationships, but from her*self*. Supporting Grace's shelter was a good first step to becoming a better version of herself.

Moving back to Nashville had been an easy decision; the implosion of her relationship splashed across the tabloid headlines certainly accelerated things. She'd needed somewhere safe to lick her wounded pride. So here she was, back at her parents' house until she figured out her next move.

Nikki interrupted her thoughts. "I've laid your clothes out for this morning. Do you want a cup of coffee?"

"I do, but you know you don't have to wait on me."

"When in Rome." Nikki stretched her arms out wide to indicate *Rome* was Krisi's family mansion. "Your parents tend to be more comfortable with the idea that I'm your maid."

Krisi scrunched her brow. "But you're not my maid. You haven't ever been." Nikki's job was to keep Krisi's world organized. She wouldn't have become the entrepreneur she was without Nikki's help.

"*I* know that and *you* know that..." Nikki shrugged. "Typically, when we come to Nashville, it's just for a few days. It's easy to overlook almost anything for a few days. This time, it's not just a visit. We're here to stay. Eventually, we may have to deal with who I am to you—your business associate."

Krisi let out a big sigh. Her parents had certain...expectations she hadn't had to deal with in years. Even though this house was massive, she wasn't sure how living here again would feel.

"Thanks, Nikki. I don't deserve you."

"True," Nikki said with a wink on her way out the door. "I'll be back shortly with your coffee."

Forty-five minutes later, Krisi scrutinized herself in an antique oval mirror, one of the few remnants of her childhood. It stood in a corner, its delicate form at odds with the heavy, intricately carved vanity next to it. Her reflection showed slim-cut pale pink pants, hemmed just above her ankles, and a matching silk shirt with embroidered flowers. It was one of her favorite outfits she'd found in Paris, and it made her feel fresh and ready to tackle the day. She kept her long blond hair straight and wore minimal makeup. Her final touch, as always, was her signature scent—*Kristine*. She spritzed it on each wrist, the pulse points of her neck, and a touch on her jacket.

Then, in a waft of citrus, vanilla, and bergamot, she picked up a lavender jacket and headed out of the room, leaving behind a mess in both the bedroom and bathroom for someone else to deal with. Her Louboutins—also pale pink with embroidered flowers—*clicked* as she made her way down the curved staircase.

"You're up early." Krisi's father, sitting at the small breakfast table, looked up from his newspaper as she rushed into the kitchen.

"Mornin', Daddy." She kissed her father on his cheek, inhaling the scent of coffee along with the sandalwood and cardamom her father had worn since her childhood. He was a handsome man and, at sixty, had aged well. His dark hair was flecked with gray at the temples, and the gym in the basement kept his body fit.

"I'm glad I caught you," he said. "Have a seat."

"Sorry, Daddy. I'm on my way to an appointment. Can I catch you later?" Krisi had the door open, ready to step out.

"Have a seat," he said again, his tone brooking no argument.

Krisi frowned as she closed the door and looked at her silver Bulgari watch. "Of course. I've...got a couple of minutes to spare." She really didn't. "What can I do for you this morning?"

"There's someone I want you to get to know at the gala."

The Nashville Charity Auction & Gala was in a couple of weeks. It was a big charity event attended by many of Nashville's elite. Her mother had spearheaded the event for years, and it was a family tradition to attend together.

"Of course. I'm happy to talk to anyone you'd like." She was used to such requests from her father.

"I'd like you to do more than just talk to Senator Michael Black."

She raised an eyebrow and chuckled. "You pimping me out, Daddy?"

"Don't be crass, Kristine."

Her spine stiffened at his tone and disgusted expression. It was unusual for him to not smile at her jokes.

"What exactly is it you'd like from me, Father?" He hated when she called him *Father*, but at the moment, he didn't feel like *Daddy*. She could see by his expression, she'd captured his full attention.

"Kristine, you've spent the last several years flitting around the globe without a care in the world. I saw the article in the *Nashville Daily* this morning about your return. I'm curious, are you planning to stay this time?" He expertly shifted the topic but kept a businesslike tone.

She rolled with the change, used to her father's style. "Yes, I'm planning to stay in Nashville."

"I'm glad to hear it." He nodded his approval and took a sip of coffee. He wasn't finished yet. "I think it's time for you to start giving back to the business and to the family paying for the extravagant lifestyle you've lived."

It seemed they'd finally reached the point of this conversation. She was curious about how it would come back to Senator Michael Black; she had no doubt it would.

"And how do you see me *giving back* to this family and the business?"

Krisi had zero desire to be part of the family business, and her father knew it. She'd been exploring her own endeavors for several years, interests she hadn't shared with her father...or many others, for that matter. She moved out more than ten years ago, and for the past five years, she'd paid for her *extravagant lifestyle*, as he called it, out of her own pocket.

It was her older brother, Alexander, who loved the family business and was being groomed to take over. Krisi doubted their father would ever willingly hand over the reins to anyone.

Her sister, Lily, home from college for the summer, sauntered into the kitchen. She was a younger version of Krisi—long blond hair, long slim body, a brain that was discarded as worthless by many. Even with her hair piled on top of her head in a messy bun and wearing pajamas under a dark purple silk robe, she was gorgeous. She dropped a kiss on their father's cheek as she made her way to the coffee pot.

"Morning, Daddy. Morning, Krisi."

Their father nodded at Lily. "Morning, princess."

Behind their father's back, Lily rolled her eyes. She hated being called *princess*.

He turned to Krisi. "I think it's time for you to settle down, time to choose an advantageous partner who—"

"An *advantageous* partner?" Krisi couldn't help interrupting him. She looked at Lily, whose eyes were wide, then back at her father. "I was thinking I would *settle down* with someone I fell in love with." While she was growing up, her father had been strict about who she dated and was seen with, but he'd never put pressure on her to *settle down*.

Her father scoffed. "Surely you realize you don't have the luxury to fall in love, Kristine. Marriages at our social level are made in boardrooms not bedrooms. And whether you like it or not, you are an asset for this family and our business. It's time to start acting like it."

So she was an asset, not just a daughter. Disappointment rippled through her. Maybe that's what was wrong with her parents' relationship. Her mother came from a wealthy family in New Orleans. Krisi wondered if *their* relationship was a merger, created in a boardroom.

But Krisi wasn't willing to be handed off to the highest bidder; she was willing to bet on love.

"This isn't about Senator Black, is it?" Lily asked, bringing Krisi back to the present. "He gives me the creeps."

"Stay out of this, Lily. It's no concern of yours." He brushed her off.

Yeah, Krisi thought wryly, *until it's time to auction* her *off to the highest bidder*. Thinking of the highest bidder, she looked at her watch and pushed her chair back. Whether her father was done or not, she was.

Just then, her mother came in, perfectly dressed with not a hair out of place—no strand would have dared.

"Good morning, Mother." Krisi nodded to her and stood.

Her mother studied her from head to toe. "Kristine, is that an outfit from Paris?" She pursed her lips while continuing to inspect Krisi. "We'll get you an appointment with Sadie for some...appropriate clothes." She sat at the table and waited for her personal maid to bring a cup of coffee. "Where are you off to so early?"

"I have a meeting with Grace Montgomery about her bachelor auction fundraiser."

Her mother raised a groomed eyebrow. "A bachelor auction? How...interesting. You might want to touch up your lipstick before leaving. Camera ready, darling."

Internally, Krisi rolled her eyes but externally nodded before heading out the kitchen door. For her few years abroad, she'd been able to forget about the pressure from her parents. She always made an effort to look put together before leaving the house, but here at home, she was never good enough. How had she forgotten that?

Krisi rushed into Music Row Joe's, impressed at being only five minutes late after being waylaid by her parents. She had taken a minute after she pulled into the parking lot to touch up her lipstick.

Joe's was a funky coffee shop a little off the beaten path, somewhere she'd never been. She looked around the colorful café and spotted Grace in a back corner. She waved before hurrying around the tables.

"Good morning." Krisi pulled out the chair opposite Grace. "I'm so sorry I'm late. My father decided today was the day he needed to have a heart-to-heart with me. And then my mother had to give me the once-over." She rolled her eyes before looking around again. The bright yellow, pink, and green decorating the small café lifted her spirits. "This is a great place. I love the guitars on the walls."

"Isn't it fun? Mama and Carl used to come here." Grace had moved to Nashville after her mother passed away. Krisi wondered if being here was comforting or hard for her. "Carl introduced me to it shortly after I moved here." She grinned. "And no problem with your timing. I just got here myself."

A server came over to their table and spoke with the slow southern drawl Krisi had missed. "Mornin', ladies."

Krisi could tell the instant the woman recognized her. Her smile bumped up a smidge, and Krisi wondered if her visit was about to be blasted on social media. Just once, it would be nice to go out and not be recognized.

"What can I get you today, ma'am?" she asked, looking at Krisi.

Krisi couldn't fault the woman. She'd grown up in the spotlight, and many of her outings and escapades had made headlines, especially here in Nashville.

She and Grace placed their orders for coffee and pastries, then continued their conversation when they were alone again.

"Is it always like that?" Grace asked, nodding toward the waitress.

"Not always, but often." Krisi sighed.

"So other than being recognized, how do you like being back in Nashville?"

"I love Nashville," Krisi said with a wistful smile. "The whole atmosphere is different than in Europe."

She'd met Grace during one of her visits home. Carl—Krisi's ex-boyfriend and Grace's new husband—had connected the two of them when Grace was looking to buy a house in the mountains. Krisi sold her cabin to Grace and made a point to keep in touch with her. Her hand absently went to her necklace to rub the lamp.

"You don't miss Paris? All those lovely French men?" Grace waggled her eyebrows and laughed.

"There are *parts* of Paris I miss," Krisi said. She missed drinking coffee on her little balcony each morning while looking at the Eiffel Tower. Flower vendors on every corner. *And...oh, the pastries*, she thought wistfully. "But the men aren't one of them. Almost every time I went out at night, the paparazzi followed. And more often than not, the men who asked me out were more interested in having their face and name splashed across newspaper pages than in me."

"Ugh," Grace groaned. "That would definitely get old. Maybe Nashville has a man who's perfect for you."

Krisi laughed. "I'm not convinced there *is* a perfect man for me."

"There is," Grace said with the assurance of a woman in love. "So how is living at your parents' place?"

Thinking back to her conversation with her father, Krisi frowned. "I thought living at my parents' house wouldn't be a big deal. I've come home for visits over the years, and it was always easy. I mean, the house is huge—you'd think it would be easy to avoid each other. But I guess moving back versus visiting is a whole different situation. One, I suppose, I wasn't prepared for." She shook her head and took a sip from the water glass in front of her. "I'm not used to my father thinking he has a say in my life. Especially my dating life. I think it's time to start looking for a place of my own in Nashville."

Grace gave her a sympathetic smile. "You looking to buy or rent?" She waved her hand, shooing away the question. "It doesn't matter. You should check out The Athenian."

The server came back and set their drinks and food on the table. "Can I get y'all anything else?"

Krisi smiled at the woman and shook her head. They each sipped their piping hot coffee and grinned.

"It may not be French roast from a Parisian café, but that's good." Krisi sighed. She turned her attention back to Grace. "I remember dropping by The Athenian at Christmas—I caught you right before you left for your wedding. It's a gorgeous building. Do you still live there?"

"No." Grace shook her head. "After the wedding, I sold Mama's penthouse to Laci Love. It's a great place, and I know Laci will take good care of it."

Grace had just gotten married at the end of December, so a little over four months earlier. She and Carl were a good match, and Krisi appreciated that Grace didn't hold anything against her regarding her past relationship with Carl. She was enjoying getting to know Grace.

"It's a great location," Krisi said, almost to herself. The idea of living downtown in a beautifully restored historic building was appealing. Very appealing. She would look into it. Well, Nikki would look into it.

Maybe, just maybe, she could keep her private life out of her father's hands.

"Brian will be able to tell you if anything's available. He knows everything that goes on there. I'm pretty sure he keeps a few apartments for renters."

After finishing her coffee and pastry, Grace spread out some papers in the center of the table..

"Okay, now to bachelor auction business. I have several men committed this year." She looked up from the list. "Actually, Brian from The Athenian is one of them. I'm hoping you can help me fill out the roster." Grace passed one of the papers to Krisi. It contained a list of the committed bachelors and another list of potentials.

"I know some of these men. I'd be happy to talk them into joining the auction. I missed it last year, so give me a rundown on how it works."

"Each bachelor will come with a planned date, and women will bid to go on that date with him. There is no commitment beyond the one date, and the bachelor can make the date whatever he's comfortable with."

Krisi nodded. "How many bachelors are you looking for?"

"Twelve seems to be a good number. Last year, we had a few more, and it went a bit long, in my opinion. So we just need a couple more."

"I can try to get my brother." Krisi grinned.

"Ooh." Grace grinned back at her. "A date with the elusive Alexander St. Claire...that would be wonderful."

"He needs balance in his life," Krisi said, still smiling. "He spends way too much time working."

"Do you want to work on him or have me approach him?"

"Why don't you approach him? If you have any trouble, let me know. He owes me."

Today was turning into an interesting day. She was definitely going to have Nikki call The Athenian to see if anything was available. She also needed to find office space for her business, since she was planning to stay.

Chapter 2

BRIAN

EARLY MONDAY MORNING, BRIAN Streatt stepped into the elevator after watching the sunrise from the rooftop and punched the button for the second floor of the sixteen-story building. His was the only apartment in use on that floor, though he knew he would probably have to fully open it up at some point. More people were inquiring about living at The Athenian. Which was a good problem, but he valued his privacy, and having the whole floor gave him not only privacy but the anonymity he desired.

If you asked the residents of The Athenian about their doorman and property manager, they'd likely tell you Brian was the friendly face of the building. He's the guy who could summon a cab or secure a reservation with a quick phone call. But they wouldn't know he lived among them. There were eight apartments on each of the lower fourteen floors, and four penthouse apartments on each of the top two floors, for a total of one hundred twenty apartments. Well, one hundred twelve, since he didn't really count the second floor.

Brian walked to the end of the hall, to the space he called home. He hadn't decorated his apartment with the luxury of the other homes in the building. Instead he'd brought the living room furniture from his parents' house and filled the rest with antique and thrift-store finds—the wood kitchen table he'd fallen in love with at an antique store hadn't come with chairs, so he'd picked up a few strays at the farmers' market. It all created a rather mishmash style.

He walked past the table into the kitchen and placed his empty coffee mug in the stainless steel dishwasher. He wiped down the gray granite counters and turned off the top-of-the-line coffee maker. He enjoyed coffee from fresh ground beans each morning. It had been his big splurge when he moved to the building.

He looked at his trusty Timex, a gift from his father only a month before both of his parents died in a car accident. With no other family, that crash had left him and his younger sister on their own. It was time to get moving, Brian realized, and he made his way to the bathroom to get ready for the day.

Thirty minutes later, he was dressed in what he thought of as his uniform. He'd gone from the camo of his military days to black trousers, a white long-sleeved button-down shirt, and a vest. Today's vest was black and purple. It was one of his favorites, a Christmas gift from his sister, Shelby. He took the stairs at the end of the hallway down to his office on the first floor.

His first task every Monday was to scan his planner to assess what the week looked like before heading out to the lobby, where the first stop on his morning rounds was always

Melody Brews Café. Melody made an excellent cup of coffee.

"Mr. Titan." Sitting at a small table by the door with a cup of black coffee, Brian greeted a gentleman entering the café.

He'd discovered this was an easy way to keep in touch with many of the residents, since so many grabbed coffee. It had become a favorite way to start his day. The only time Brian saw Mr. Titan out of his apartment was to get his morning coffee.

"Brian." The man greeted him with a nod before making his way to the counter where Melody waited. After ordering, he stepped back to Brian's table. "How's the cleanup going in Harry's old apartment?"

Harry, a longtime renter, had moved out recently, leaving an empty apartment on the sixth floor.

"I've got a crew coming in either today or tomorrow to finish painting, and the new appliances go in on Friday."

Mr. Titan nodded. "Are you going to get another renter? Or sell it this time? Harry was a good neighbor. He never bothered me."

Brian grinned. Xavier Titan was a best-selling suspense author who wrote at odd hours and didn't like being bothered by his neighbors. Well, by anyone.

"I'm not sure, but I'll let you know."

When his name was called, Mr. Titan walked back to the counter, picked up his insulated to-go cup, then nodded to Brian on his way out the door.

Melody came over with a full carafe and topped off his cup. The older woman had become a staple in the community he'd created. Like him, she knew all the residents by name and kept up with their lives. He appreciated her gentle way of caring for his residents.

Twenty minutes later, with an empty cup in front of him, Brian waved to Melody and made his way out of the shop. Checking in with each of the businesses on the first floor of The Athenian was a part of his Monday routine before he settled in behind the desk. During his military days, he'd learned to appreciate routine and order, and he'd carried it over to The Athenian. It was important to know everything was running smoothly.

A year earlier, it had been his project to fill the empty first floor spaces with businesses he thought would not only benefit the building's residents but would also thrive in downtown Nashville. He promoted the businesses to the residents in their monthly newsletter, and it was satisfying to see them grow.

Directly across from Melody Brews Café was Nashville Uncorked, an upscale wine bar that would open later in the day, and next door was Billie's Books & Such. A bookstore was a risky business venture, but it had quickly become a favorite for residents and walk-in traffic alike. Billie did a good job stocking what her customers wanted.

"Mornin', Billie." The scent of new books, candles, and fresh coffee from next door greeted him, making him smile.

"Oh. Good morning, Brian." A flustered Billie stood at the counter with a big pile of boxes and spoke to a young woman. After finishing her conversation, she picked up a coffee mug—it read *I like big books!*—and joined Brian by the new release table.

"How's it going today, boss?" In a move that was so ingrained she probably didn't even realize she was doing it, Billie started rearranging and straightening books on the table.

"Goin' good. Nice mug." He chuckled and nodded to her coffee cup. "How's it going here? You looked a little frazzled when I came in."

"Oh." She rolled her eyes. "We got a shipment last night, one we've been waiting for...except it doesn't have anything I ordered." She put her hands up and shrugged. "Some days, it's so annoying to be the boss."

"You'll get it straightened out." It was unusual to see Billie upset. Brian nodded toward the young woman unboxing books at the counter. "I'm happy to see you finally got some help."

"Yeah, it's a relief to be able to afford help for the summer. And thanks. I appreciate your confidence in me. I'm just a little overwhelmed at the moment." Billie grinned. "Oh hey, I'm hosting a book club this summer. I'll bring in local authors for readings, book signings, and such. I'm excited—we already have a few authors signed on."

"That sounds like a fun project. Have you talked to our in-house author, Mr. Titan, yet?"

She shivered dramatically. "Heck no. He scares me. Always so unfriendly. I don't think I've ever had a full conversation with the man. But," she continued, moving the conversation away from the grumpy author, "I'm working with Graham at Uncorked. He's going to provide wine and nibbles for each event. It's coming together nicely."

"That's great, Billie. Let me know when you've got the schedule figured out, and I'll do an email blast to the residents," Brian offered. He nodded toward the stack of boxes. "I'll let you get back to it. Good luck." He stepped back into the hallway and waved goodbye.

Across the hall, he opened the door to the Nirvana Spa, where he was greeted by dim lighting and a scent that took him back to his grandmother's house. He had no idea what it was, but he knew it was the perfume his grandmother had worn all the time.

"Morning, Sharla." He greeted the woman behind the counter. "What's the scent this morning?"

She grinned at him. "It's a rosewater blend. You like it?"

"It reminds me of my grandmother."

"Hmm...I'm not sure I want patrons thinking of grandmothers," she said with a slight frown. "I was hoping for more of a summer-day-in-the-garden feel."

He grinned. "Well, I'm sure others will think just that. Everything okay today?"

"Yep, I have a full schedule. Mostly residents, but I'm starting to get downtown folks wanderin' in."

"That's great," Brian said. "Glad it's going well."

The bell tinkled, and Brian held the door open for a woman.

"Have a great day," he said as he returned to the hallway and took a deep breath. The sweet scent had always given him a headache when he was a kid, and he wasn't interested in sticking around to see if he'd grown out of it.

It pleased him, though, to hear The Athenian businesses were growing. It was good for everyone. He opened another door to poke his head into the pet spa and froze. A small dog, yapping and running around and dragging a leash, darted past him and out the door with Denise, the pet spa owner, and another woman, presumably the dog's owner, right behind.

"Mornin', Brian," Denise said as she rushed past, her long brown ponytail bouncing behind her.

He watched her bright pink scrubs with monkeys swinging across them disappear down the hallway. "Um, do you need help?" he called, unsure what to do other than watch the chaos.

"No, we got it," Denise yelled over her shoulder.

He stood for another minute holding the door, then closed it and followed their path to the lobby. Just as he passed the last business, an art gallery, Athenian Canvas Collective, the harried dog owner passed him on her way back to the pet spa, a squirming dog in her grasp.

Denise followed behind. "Nothin' to see here," she joked as she passed.

He grinned and shook his head, relieved the chaos was under control, before continuing to his office. While he spent a lot of time at the small desk in the lobby, most of his work was done in the office behind it.

The Athenian was his baby, and making sure it ran well and the residents were happy were his primary concerns. He loved what he did. He enjoyed being part of the community he'd created. He'd built a comfortable life for himself and his sister.

Did he want more? Sure, sometimes. He felt guilty wanting more when everything was so good. But...it would be nice to have someone to share the sunrise with. Share his life with.

It wouldn't happen anytime soon. His purpose in life right now was to take care of Shelby. And The Athenian.

Two hours later, Brian shut down his computer and pushed back from the desk. With the finances in order, he was ready to deal with Monday errands. Specifically, he needed to fill his fridge since Shelby was coming home for the summer.

As if on cue, his cell phone vibrated, signaling a call. "Shelby," he said. "How's my favorite sister?"

Her laughter at the old joke always made him smile. "I'm your only sister, silly. How's my favorite *older* brother?"

Her emphasis on the word *older* always made him grin. With twelve years between them, it wasn't surprising she thought he was old.

"I'm good. I was just heading to the farmers' market to fill up the fridge for your bottomless pit of a stomach."

"Excellent." Shelby's energy and enthusiasm for life came through the phone line.

"When will you and all your belongings descend on Nashville?"

"I took my last final today and should be there by noon tomorrow, depending on what time I wake up. I hope to be on the road by eight, so let's plan on having lunch together."

"I will gladly take you to lunch." He grinned again as they signed off. Even though her arrival would put his orderly life and apartment in complete chaos, he was looking forward to having her around.

Pushing open the door at the back of his office, he ran up the stairs to his apartment. In his bedroom, he changed into a pair of jeans, pulled on a plain white T-shirt, and grabbed his leather jacket on the way out. After a quick scan of the refrigerator, he made his way back down the stairs, locked up his office, and took the side door to the garage.

The black truck in the closest parking space was his, but his favorite way to get around the city, especially in the spring, was to ride his motorcycle. Brian put on the jacket and helmet, stowed his shopping bags, then swung his leg over his silver-and-black Shadow Phantom.

It purred as he pulled out of the underground garage and onto Demonbreun Street. He rode past the Country Music Hall of Fame and kept going past the capitol. He lifted the visor on his helmet to enjoy the fresh cool air hitting his face as he slowly made his way across town.

The Nashville Farmers' Market wasn't even two miles from The Athenian, but traffic always made the trip longer than expected. He parked his bike in a space designated for motorcycles near the entrance, attached his helmet to the handlebars, and grabbed his shopping bags from the storage compartment on the back of the bike.

The farmers' market was one of Brian's favorite places. Every week offered a new experience, depending on which vendors were there. He had his favorites, but it was fun to check out what was new.

He ran his hands through his helmet hair, tucked his sunglasses into his shirt, and walked past the food trucks and into the building. He typically stopped by on Saturdays to pick up fresh produce, but on his Monday visits, he took longer and visited his favorite indoor stalls. He liked to start in the artisan craft area and finish in the food court, where he would pick up meals for the week and eat lunch.

Chapter 3

KRISI

WITH A CRITICAL EYE, Krisi looked herself over in her bedroom mirror. The jeans were a little baggy, and the flannel shirt looked out of place on her body, but it felt good. So soft. *This is an absurd idea*, she told herself for the hundredth time. But it was just one day. One afternoon. And after the confrontation with her parents and the newspaper article, the notion that she could be someone else, even for a brief time, was tempting.

"I don't know, Krisi." Nikki stood behind her shaking her head. "This seems foolish."

Krisi grinned at the woman who'd been her friend through thick and thin and could undoubtedly read her mind. "You're probably right, Nikki, but I certainly don't look like *me*, do I?"

She looked again at her reflection. The outfit belonged to Nikki, including the beat-up athletic shoes. Krisi's long blond ponytail was hidden beneath a ball cap.

"If my mother could see me..." Krisi rolled her eyes at her own reflection.

When she got home from her appointment with Grace, her mother had already made an appointment for Krisi with her stylist. She complained the clothes Krisi wore in Paris weren't appropriate for Nashville, and it was time to update her wardrobe. After all, it was important to *dress to impress.*

When Krisi lived here before, ten years ago, her life had been filled with social commitments—luncheons, fundraisers, shopping. She escaped to Europe to see what else life had to offer.

She turned away from the mirror and walked into her sitting room. Nikki followed and sat in the chair next to her.

"Now, where can I go where no one will recognize me?"

Nikki shook her head, a wry grin on her face. "Why don't you go to the farmers' market? It's always interesting."

Krisi thought about it. She'd never been to the Nashville Farmers' Market. In Europe, she and Nikki often visited local markets filled with fresh fruit, vegetables, flowers, and wine. Dinner was based on what they found each day.

"That could be fun. I doubt I'll run into anyone I know. Mother certainly won't be there to see that I'm not *camera ready*." She emphasized the last two words with air quotes.

"It's a great place to wander," Nikki said.

"Perfect." Krisi was warming up to the idea. She wanted to peruse the market incognito for a couple of hours. No press. No family obligation. Just herself.

"Daddy's at his office and Mother is at the spa. I think I'll order a rideshare so I won't have to worry about driving." She pulled out her phone and put in her order on the app, then turned back to Nikki. "Can I bring back anything for you?"

Nikki grinned. "Sure. Bring anything you like for me."

Krisi knew Nikki thought she was being silly, but she couldn't help being excited. Based on her experiences in Europe, she was delighted by the idea of looking through fresh produce, and maybe she'd find flowers to brighten up her room.

The idea of going somewhere and not being recognized, though, was even more appealing. That, and not popping up in the society page of the paper again. She just wanted to live life. At least for today.

Her phone dinged, alerting her that her driver had arrived. She picked up a jean jacket, pulled her cap a little lower, and headed for the door. "I'll be back shortly."

"Don't get in any trouble." Nikki chuckled.

Krisi rolled her eyes as she walked out the door but couldn't keep the grin off her face. She went outside and found her driver waiting next to a small white sedan.

The drive to the farmers' market was un-
eventful, and Krisi was dropped off at the entrance. The building in front of her was completely unexpected. Truth be told, she hadn't
known what to expect, but her thoughts had
been more along the line of tents with trays of
fruits and vegetables, not this huge building.

As she walked through the entrance, a
whole new world was laid out before her,
with an enchanting and lively atmosphere.
She stopped to take in the vibrant colors
of fresh flowers, artisanal goods, and the
bustling crowd. Not only was the air scent-
ed with flowers, but the heady smell of food
made her stomach grumble. She hadn't expected restaurants.

She couldn't help but smile as she strolled
through the vendor stalls. There was everything from handcrafted jewelry to lemon
trees. Not at all what she'd been expecting.
Intrigued by a display, Krisi smiled at the
woman behind the table and picked up a
rough-cut bar with small dark purple lavender buds poking out of the soap. "These are
lovely. Goat milk?"

The woman smiled back at Krisi. "Thank you. Yes, all of our soaps are handcrafted using goat milk and other natural ingredients." She nodded to the bar Krisi was holding. "That one is a blend of lavender and eucalyptus. It has a calming yet refreshing aroma, don't you think?"

Krisi held the bar to her nose, enjoying the opportunity to speak with someone who worked with scents. "I love this combination." She sniffed the bar again. "Is there some...cedarwood in there too?"

The woman arched a brow. "There is, just a touch."

Krisi smiled. "It's lovely." She kept the bar in her hand while looking at the other offerings.

"Ah, well, a lot of experimentation goes into each soap. I draw inspiration from nature, my surroundings, sometimes even from memories. Each scent has its own story to tell, so I keep a scent notebook to write down any thoughts, combinations, or even images that come to me."

Krisi smiled at the woman. She had a similar notebook tucked into her purse...and she would be adding to it before the day was done. "I find myself drawn to scents with a backstory." She gave an awkward laugh, a little chagrined by what she'd shared, but the woman across from her nodded sagely.

"I completely understand what you mean," she said. "You work with scents too." It wasn't a question.

Krisi hadn't wanted to share about herself today, but she really enjoyed talking with this woman. "I work in perfumes, so like you, I tend to experiment with a lot of different scent combinations." She held the soap up again. "These work so well together."

"Thank you." The woman was clearly proud of her soaps and happy to share about them. "We source local herbs and essential oils to create unique blends. No synthetic fragrances or harsh chemicals. We aim to give a luxurious, gentle experience."

Krisi looked at the woman. "That sounds amazing, and your designs are gorgeous."

"I'm so glad you like them. Each batch is crafted with care. This is my newest one." She handed a beautiful pale yellow bar to Krisi. "I call it Citrus Burst."

Krisi held the bar up to her nose and closed her eyes. It reminded her of her own scent, the signature scent created solely for her. Hers had bergamot and vanilla while the soap had something she couldn't identify.

"Oh, this is wonderful! Invigorating and refreshing. I definitely need a couple of these. Do you take credit cards?"

"Absolutely." The woman wrapped the bars in tissue paper and put them in a small pale green bag with the name of her business on it. "My sister is a few stalls down and has handmade candles with similar scents. You should stop by."

Thirty minutes later, after she'd filled multiple bags with soaps, candles, and lotions, Krisi's mind was reeling with collaboration ideas. She tucked the thoughts away and wandered further until she found herself in front of a bakery stall. The scent of freshly baked bread nearly overwhelmed her. Stepping into the line, she decided to pick up a few loaves to share with Nikki along with the soap, lotion, and candle she'd bought for her.

As she stood in line, a young boy captured her attention, his big eyes fixed on the display. She understood the hungry look in his eyes. She couldn't wait to taste the olive focaccia she planned to order. When she finally made it to the front of the line, she asked for several types of bread. She looked over at the boy, who was still staring at the display.

"Would you like that?" she asked. At his nod, she pulled down a loaf and handed it to him. His gap-toothed grin made her smile, then he ran off with the loaf. "You can add that loaf to my bill." It felt good to share this experience with the young boy.

The baker came over with a bag loaded with the different breads and set it on the counter in front of her. "That'll be thirty-five dollars, please."

She reached into her purse and pulled out her credit card. It was getting more use than she'd expected.

"I'm sorry, miss, I don't take cards," the man behind the counter said.

"Oh, I..." Krisi fumbled in her purse and began to panic as she scoured her wallet. "I'm sorry, I don't have cash. I rarely carry any."

"I only take cash." The large man stood with his hands on his hips. "No cash, no bread." He started to reach for the bag.

"I'm sorry. I..." This was so humiliating. The first time she goes out as a *real* person, and she can't pay for her own bread. "Let me call a friend and have her bring cash."

"I got this." A man behind her handed the vendor two twenties.

Krisi turned to stare at him. He was tall, probably six-foot-two or -three, with a body belonging to a football player. His worn jeans fit him well, snug in all the right places, and under his black leather jacket, his simple white T-shirt stretched across broad shoulders. She bit her lower lip and wondered just who her rescuer was

Her cheeks heated up. "I'm so embarrassed. Thank you. How can I repay you?"

"Ah, don't worry about it."

She enjoyed his soft southern drawl and flushed cheeks. He turned his attention to the vendor and placed his own order. He turned back to Krisi. "It was nice of you to buy that boy some bread."

"Well, turns out, it was *you* who actually bought it." She closed her eyes and shook her head. "I can't believe I didn't think to bring cash."

The man brushed past her discomfort. "I see that boy here frequently but don't know his story." The man looked around, then turned back to her. "Have you had lunch yet? I was going to grab a bite to eat."

"As long as we find a place that takes credit cards." She grinned wryly. "I'll buy."

The idea of having lunch with this very handsome man who didn't want anything from her was appealing. She could just be herself. She couldn't remember the last time she was able to just be herself with a man.

Chapter 4

BRIAN

BRIAN WASN'T USED TO paying for someone else's order, but something about seeing the woman in front of him scramble as she searched through her purse touched his heart. He wasn't sure why the interaction didn't end there, but now he was leading her through the market to his favorite food stall, Nashville Chaat, which featured Indian food. He hadn't planned on sharing lunch with a beautiful woman today, but he wasn't disappointed his plans had changed.

"Indian food okay?" He probably should have asked earlier.

"Sure, why not? Today is all about new experiences." She grinned.

"By the way, I'm Brian." He shuffled his packages around and held out his hand to her.

"Krisi," she said, taking his hand in hers.

Her hand was small and soft, but it was the tingling warmth running up his arm that caught his attention. By the look on her face and how quickly she let go, he wondered if she felt it too.

They joined the queue and silently watched the vendor swiftly and precisely attend to each order. Eventually, they made their way to the front of the line.

"Brian," the man cheerfully greeted him. "Always good to see you, my friend, especially when you bring a beautiful woman with you." His thick eyebrows wiggled.

Brian felt his cheeks warm. "Arnav, this is my new friend, Krisi." He looked at her and was relieved to see a big smile on her face. "Krisi, meet the incorrigible Arnav."

Arnav laughed and turned to Krisi. "What can I get you, pretty lady?"

She grinned at Brian, then looked at the man. "I'm not sure. What do you recommend?"

"Definitely the pani puri. You will enjoy the burst of flavors." Without waiting for her consent, he began preparing her meal. "And you, my friend?" He looked at Brian. "Your usual?"

Brian nodded, his stomach growling with anticipation. He sure hoped Krisi liked bold, flavorful food, otherwise this wouldn't go well. Within a couple of minutes, they had their food and he led her through the maze of stalls to a large open space with picnic tables.

They found an empty table and settled across from each other. Something about this woman's face was familiar, but he couldn't put his finger on it.

"I never forget a face," Brian said after they settled. "I feel like I've met you before, but I can't place when or where."

She squirmed a bit and looked uncomfortable. "I've not been here before, so I doubt we've met."

He thought about the way her hand felt in his and knew they hadn't been introduced when he'd previously seen her. When and where was still a mystery, but he let it go, deciding to ruminate on it later. For now, he was having lunch with a beautiful woman who piqued his interest. It hadn't happened for way too long.

"Oh my gosh."

Krisi's voice broke into his thoughts.

"This food is amazing! He wasn't kidding when he said it was a burst of flavor. So good."

Brian grinned at her. "That's a relief. Not everyone is cut out for bold flavors."

"I've had, apparently, only poor imitations of Indian food before. This…" She took another bite.

Brian enjoyed her enthusiasm.

"You mentioned you hadn't been to the farmers' market before," Brian said. "What brought you here today?"

She paused before answering, as if trying to decide what to say. "I recently moved back to Nashville and wanted to get out to explore a bit. A friend recommended I come here…so here I am. How about you? It sounds like you're a regular?"

"I'm not much of a cook, so I typically come on Monday to fill up my fridge." He was embarrassed about how rarely he used the gorgeous kitchen back in his apartment. "I got a call from my younger sister this morning, and she'll be home tomorrow for the summer." At Krisi's questioning expression, he continued, "Shelby's in college. She just finished her junior year." He looked at his plate. "She'll be the first in our family to graduate from college."

"Did you go straight into the workforce?" There didn't appear to be any judgment in her question, just curiosity.

"I wound up going the military route." He'd taken to military life, and prior to his parents' accident, he'd been planning to sign up for another stint. The regimented routine was good for him. He still found that an orderly routine brought comfort.

"You must be so proud of her. How old is she?" Krisi pushed her empty plate aside and leaned forward. Interested.

"Shelby's amazing. She's making straight As." His face flushed again. He needed to stop babbling. "Sorry. I'm just so proud of her. To answer your question, she's twenty-two."

"I have a twenty-two-year-old sister too." Krisi gave him a faint smile. "My parents thought they were done, so she was a huge surprise."

"A happy surprise?" Brian asked, thinking about his parents' joyful reaction to Shelby's arrival. He regretted the question immediately. It felt too personal to ask someone he'd just met.

Krisi blew out a breath. "I suppose it depends on who you ask. My mother thought she was done and wasn't thrilled. She's never been a very...hands-on mom, I guess you could say. But my father makes up for it by overindulging Lily. She's his princess." She chuckled at that. "She hates when he calls her *princess*. Lily's a lot of fun. My brother and I adore her."

Brian wondered if they were close like he and Shelby. Just then, his phone buzzed with an alarm. He glanced down and was stunned to see they'd spent over an hour talking.

"I'm really sorry, but I have to get to work." He stood up and started collecting their trash.

She glanced at her thin silver watch. "Oh gracious. I need to head back too."

He walked to the can across the room and dumped their trash. When he returned to the table, she was frowning at her phone.

"Something wrong?"

"I forgot to schedule my ride home, and now it's going to be an hourlong wait for a car to arrive."

"I don't mind dropping you off, if you're comfortable riding with me?" She only had a few small bags, and they would easily fit into the saddle bags on his motorcycle.

Frowning again, she looked like she was having an internal debate. "Thank you, but I don't want to put you out. I can just wait." She didn't look happy about her decision.

"It's no problem. I'm happy to drop you off wherever you need to go."

She looked at him. "Are you sure?"

Brian really wanted to give her a ride home. He wasn't ready to say goodbye. "Like I said, not a problem at all."

"Well, all right then. Thank you."

She snapped a picture of him and appeared to send it to someone. Frankly, he didn't blame her; he'd want Shelby to do the same.

They picked up their bags, and he led her through the exit to the side where he'd parked his bike. He opened one of the saddle bags and organized his meals and groceries before opening the other and turning to her. She was standing several feet away with wide eyes.

"That's a motorcycle," she said.

He looked at his bike then back at her. "Yes. I guess I should have mentioned that. Is it a problem?" It hadn't occurred to him to mention he was on his bike today.

"I..." She walked a little closer. "I've never ridden on a motorcycle."

"I'm a very safe driver."

She seemed to be having another internal debate, so he waited patiently until she decided.

She stepped closer. "No, of course it's not a problem. No problem at all."

"Great." He couldn't keep the grin off his face. He took her bags and carefully loaded them in the storage compartment, then handed her his helmet. "Here, you can use this."

She reluctantly took off her baseball cap, and a long blond ponytail escaped to fall down her back. She pulled the helmet over the ponytail. It was too big for her head, but it was the only helmet he'd brought. He carefully fastened the strap under her chin before swinging his leg over the bike.

When he turned back to her, she was staring at the bike again.

"So step here"—he pointed to a footrest—"and then climb on."

She nodded and came to the bike. She put a foot on the support but then seemed unsure where to put her hands.

"You can put a hand on my shoulder," he said.

She nodded, laid a hand softly on his shoulder, and swung her leg over the bike before settling herself behind him. She'd been careful to leave a couple of inches between them.

"You're probably going to want to put your arms around my waist to hang on." He kept his face forward so she couldn't see his smile.

"Oh...no," she said, her voice rather tight. "I'm fine."

"Okay," he chuckled. "Then maybe hang onto the bar behind you."

He caught her nod in the side mirror, and watched her hands go behind her back as he started the engine. He walked the bike out of the space, then shifted into gear and slowly started forward. Within seconds, he felt Krisi's arms around his waist, making him grin.

She'd given him an address in Belle Meade and said she was staying with a friend. It was an easy drive, and he enjoyed the sensation of her body against his back. About midway through the drive, he felt her relax, her grip on his waist loosening a bit. He hoped she was enjoying the ride. In the back of his mind, he already hoped she'd want to do this again.

He didn't spend much time in Belle Meade, but it was a beautiful area. His GPS led them to a house he'd seen in the news-paper before—the St. Claire Mansion. It was even more impressive in person. Tall white columns lined the entryway with rows and rows of sparkling windows adorning all three floors. He pulled the bike up to the front steps and turned the motor off. He waited for Krisi to get off, then he put the kickstand down and swung his leg over.

He unbuckled the strap under her chin and waited while she pulled the helmet from her head. Her ponytail was wild, and her eyes were wide and bright.

"That was incredible," she said in a breathy voice. Her face glowed with excite-ment as she smashed the ballcap back onto her head.

He grinned, putting the helmet on the seat. "I'm glad you enjoyed it. It's my favorite way to get around the city." He walked to the back of the motorcycle and opened the com-partment holding her bags, happy to see they hadn't become wrinkled during the ride.

"Thank you." She reached up, her eyes twinkling, and gave him a brief kiss on the cheek, then rushed around the side of the house.

Confused, he stood staring at the corner of the house where she'd disappeared and his hand automatically went to his cheek where her lips had touched. That was weird. No goodbye, just thanks. And a kiss.

He wondered about her friend who lived at the St. Claire Mansion as he put his helmet on and got back on his bike. As he sped back the driveway, he missed the warmth of her body on his back.

He grinned all the way to the highway and back into downtown. He'd hoped to get a phone number from her, or maybe a last name so he could look her up. What he really wanted was dinner with her, but what he got was nothing.

Well, not nothing.

He got a kiss.

It wasn't much, but his cheek still tingled where her lips had touched. He had no idea how to find her again. Maybe fate would be kind and put her in his path again.

The next day, Brian found himself sitting at Nash Nosh, enjoying lunch with a woman—his sister this time. He sat back in his chair and looked at her. Her pale blond hair had grown a bit since Christmas. The blue in her eyes was a gift from their father's gene pool. She looked like she'd dropped a few pounds, and her face was thin. She was losing the "child" look he was used to. He sighed, his little sister was growing up right before his eyes.

When their parents died five years earlier, Brian became her guardian. It was a role he took very seriously. He made sure she finished high school and went to college, like their parents dreamed of. He also made sure they talked about their parents and how they were each handling their grief. It was good for both of them to have someone to remember with.

"Mr. Harry moved out? He was nice. I'll miss him and his little pug." She frowned at the news.

"Apparently, he moved in with his daughter somewhere up in Minnesota." Brian loved when Shelby came home. Her interest in the residents and businesses matched his own. She was the only person on the planet he could be completely open with. She knew all of his secrets. The only other person he'd shared his past with was a former resident, Marilyn, but she'd passed away a while ago.

Shelby took another bite. "So you going to rent his place out?"

"Mr. Titan asked that same question." He chuckled at her inquisitiveness. "To answer the question, I had a woman stop by yesterday afternoon—Nikki McAllister. She filled out the paperwork and put a deposit down for Harry's place without batting an eye. It sounds like her boss will be living there. They'll be moving in on Saturday, so we'll see who shows up."

Shelby raised an eyebrow. "Hmm. Wonder who the boss is...maybe he'll be a hot young billionaire I can have a summer fling with."

Brian almost choked on the water he'd just drunk. He held up a finger while he coughed, then wiped his eyes before shaking his head.

"Geez, Shelb...I don't want to hear about your summer flings. You're my little sister."

She grinned and he knew it was exactly the response she'd been aiming for.

"Speaking of flings, any interesting women in your life?"

He thought about Krisi but shook his head. "Not really."

Shelby narrowed her eyes and tilted her head. "You've met someone." It was a statement, not a question.

"No...well, yes. But we won't be seeing each other again."

"Why ever not?"

Brian grinned at her nosiness. "We didn't exchange numbers, so that makes it a challenge to find her"

"Too bad," Shelby said seriously. "I like the way your eyes lit up when you thought about her."

Sometimes, Brian thought, Shelby was too observant. He wished he'd gotten Krisi's number, because he liked the way his insides lit up thinking about her. Life was cruel sometimes.

Chapter 5

KRISI

SUNDAY MORNING SUN SPILLED through the expansive windows making up half a wall in Krisi's new bedroom, teasing her into waking earlier than she wanted. Of course it was her own fault. She should have closed the drapes the night before. But it had been her first night in her new apartment at The Athenian, and she hadn't been thinking about how ridiculously early the sun comes up when she crawled into bed.

She angrily threw off the covers and walked over to the windows. She was about to slam the curtains shut and hop back into bed, but the view in front of her stopped her in her tracks.

It had been years since she'd seen sunrise. Even longer since she'd seen it over the Cumberland Mountains.

Deciding sleep was no longer an option, she donned a long pink silk robe and walked out to her balcony. She didn't bother sitting in one of the lounge chairs, and instead she stood at the railing, high above the city, mesmerized by the ever-changing canvas in front of her.

Her hand instinctively reached for her necklace, and her fingers found the genie's lamp and slowly rubbed the warm charm.

- *I want to know for sure that I made the right decision moving into The Athenian.*

- *Help me build a strong community of friends I can trust.*

- *Coffee.*

Her fingers lingered a few minutes longer as she remembered the day her grandmother had given her the necklace. Krisi had been sixteen, and she and her grandmother were in London, just the two of them. During afternoon tea at Harrods the day before returning to Nashville, her grandmother slid a small silver box across the table. Krisi had been delighted to see the shiny genie's lamp charm at the end of a gold chain. She'd been young enough to still be a little fanciful and took her grandmother's instructions to heart.

Every morning, close your eyes and make three wishes.

Her grandmother told her money couldn't buy happiness and to use her wishes each morning to fill her heart. So even at thirty-two, she took some time to think about what was important and how she wanted her day to go.

Breathing in the cool early morning air, she caught the heady scent of coffee drifting to her. Taunting her. She wondered who else was up so early and wished she had a warm mug in her hand. But coffee would have to wait. The sky was coming alive with splashes of violet and indigo at the edge of the horizon, highlighting the dark outline of mountains in the distance and the city around her.

She looked at the city she loved. The city where she'd grown up before abandoning it for so many years. She turned to the south, toward the St. Claire mansion. Her family home. She'd shared the news of her move to The Athenian with her parents Friday evening. Her mother had been silent, as expected, but her father's reaction surprised her. He threatened to cut her off from family funds. When she said she was still moving, he made a show of getting up from the table, then and there, to call Mr. Abernathy, the family accountant, to make sure she wouldn't get another dime of family money. She wondered if Mr. Abernathy informed her father she hadn't used any of her father's money in over five years.

She'd created Scent SCK after finishing four years at Givaudan, the famous perfumery school in Paris. She met Gilles, a fragrance designer, shortly after graduating. Initially, she'd only wanted to create a scent for herself, but the more she and Gilles had talked, the more scents they created together, the more it made sense to start a company. He was still her perfume designer, and they met annually to create five new scents to debut the following year.

Her scent, the original, was still exclusive to her.

Her parents hadn't known about her four years at Givaudan. The only person she'd told in her family was her grandmother, who'd passed away in her third year of training, leaving her a substantial trust fund to help start her business. It wasn't public knowledge that she owned Scent SCK. She promoted it on social media, but most of the public assumed she was just a fan. Which, of course, she was.

Between her business and the trust fund, she was a wealthy woman in her own right and didn't need to dip into the family coffers to maintain her lifestyle.

It hurt that her father felt he could control her through money. She wasn't sure where that left their relationship. He'd never been one to encourage her to use her brain or become a businesswoman, which left very little for them to talk about.

She shook her head to escape her memories and looked down at the streets, cloaked in the dim light of early morning. The city was beginning to come alive. It amazed her how much activity there was at five-thirty on a weekend morning. Why the heck were all these people even awake? She could see taillights already heading into the day.

She pulled her gaze from the streets, back to the horizon. The palette in front of her had already evolved again, now soft pinks, oranges, and golds. The colors deepened as the sun crept higher in the sky. In an instant, a dazzling display surrounded her as sunlight reflected off the glass facades making up downtown. In the blink of an eye, the sky—the day—transitioned from dawn to morning. The sun was fully above the horizon, and the city below was waking up.

Turning toward her bedroom, Krisi realized she didn't want to go back to bed. She was up, ready to embrace the day ahead. From what she'd just seen, it was going to be a nice day.

She padded to her new kitchen on a mission to find coffee. The wide-plank wood floors were warm under her bare feet. The kitchen was filled with sleek, high-end, state-of-the-art appliances she had no idea how to use. Growing up with a maid, a cook, and a housekeeper had done nothing to prepare her for living alone. In Europe, Nikki had lived with her and done all the cooking. Krisi opened the dark wood cabinet above the coffee maker, hoping to find the beans, but instead of coffee, the cabinet was filled with mugs. She chose one and set it on the gleaming granite counter. One by one, she opened each cabinet and realized just how long it had been since she'd made a pot for herself. Usually, Nikki had it made by the time Krisi woke up. She grinned to herself. Nikki would be shocked when she arrived at nine to see Krisi had already been up for hours.

Krisi let out a sigh when her search ended with no coffee. Nikki had unpacked the kitchen since she was the one who knew how to use the appliances. Krisi had no idea what she would have done with coffee anyway. Deciding her next option was to head to the lobby for a cup from the café there, she made her way back to her bedroom to get dressed.

Sifting through the racks of clothes in her closet, Krisi sighed as she realized just how incredibly spoiled she was. She was so used to Nikki laying out clothes for her day, it had been months since she rifled through her own closet.

The decision to move back to Nashville had been somewhat rash. She'd been frustrated with how her relationship ended. Sick of the paparazzi following her. Sick of the men she dated. Sick of the shallow relationships surrounding her. She hoped to create more meaningful connections here, to create a life she could love.

Thirty minutes later, Krisi stepped out of the elevator in a pair of cream-colored wide-leg slacks and a bright yellow blouse. The scent of coffee greeted her, luring her down the hallway to the other end of the lobby. Melody Brews was a siren calling to her.

Krisi walked into the café and looked around. It was intimate and inviting without being cramped. The chalkboard menu on an exposed brick wall behind the counter listed daily specials, and the other walls were pale yellow, giving the place a cheerful feel.

"Good morning." The woman behind the counter smiled at her. Her bobbed haircut was more gray than brown, and her purple polo shirt with Melody Brews sewn on matched violet streaks peeking through her hair.

Krisi walked up to the counter. "Morning." She looked up at the chalkboard, overwhelmed by choices.

"What can I getcha today?"

"I'm not even sure where to start. Everything looks so good." Krisi was in the mood for something special, something to celebrate her new location, her new home.

"Ahh, you're new. I'm Melody, the owner. Welcome to Melody Brews." She grinned at Krisi. "So what is it you're looking for this morning?"

Krisi laughed. "I'm in desperate need of coffee."

"I can definitely help there. Do you like your coffee straight up? Or do you want something a little fancier?"

Looking back at the menu, Krisi frowned. "I'd like something fun and fancy, but you have so many options."

Melody nodded knowingly. "Do you like chocolate?" At Krisi's nod, she continued, "I have just the thing. How about a Music City Mocha?"

Krisi laughed. "I have no idea what that is but bring it on."

"You got it. Are you a resident?"

Krisi nodded. "I just moved in yesterday."

"Welcome to The Athenian. Glad to have you here. Brian seems to have a knack for finding the right people for our little family here." At Krisi's confused look, she said, "You've met Brian, right?"

Krisi shook her head. "You're the first person I've met here."

"Hmm, I'm surprised you didn't meet him when you filled out the paperwork or when you moved in."

"Oh, Nikki, my PA, did all that for me, bless her. I came yesterday afternoon, just in time to unpack everything."

"Gotcha. Well, I'm sure you'll meet Brian soon enough. He's the guy in charge around here, so if you need anything, he's the one you'll need to go to."

"Oh, great. Thanks. I'll make sure I meet him then."

One of the perks, Krisi discovered, of living at The Athenian was running a tab with the first floor businesses. She loved that. Turning from the counter, she scanned the room for a table. She grinned as she realized tables were readily available at this hour. There was a small two-top in the back corner by an inviting bookshelf, so she made her way there to sit down.

A few minutes later, Melody came over with an oversized, bright yellow mug topped with cinnamon-sprinkled whipped cream. "One Music City Mocha for you." Melody smiled as she set the cup on the table.

The scent of rich chocolate and strong coffee greeted Krisi as she lifted the mug. With the first sip, she knew she'd made the right choice. The mocha was decadent with rich, dark chocolate and caramel. What made it perfect was a dash of Tennessee whiskey.

Melody said, "As a welcome to the family, I thought you might like a raspberry-lemon scone to go with your coffee this morning."

Krisi looked at the triangular treat on the plate in front of her. Bright red raspberries peeked out from under glaze artfully drizzled across the top. Her stomach grumbled just looking at it. She looked up sheepishly. "I guess I'm hungry." Looking back down at the treat, she asked, "You have bakery goodies every morning?"

Melody nodded.

"I may need to get up early every morning. My waistline doesn't thank you, but the rest of me does."

Melody laughed as she walked back to the counter.

One bite of scone and Krisi knew she'd be coming in on a regular basis. The tangy sweetness of the glaze mingled nicely with the tart raspberries. Even though she'd been blessed with a good metabolism, this treat was totally worth the extra thirty minutes in the gym. She lifted her cup and let the dark, bitter coffee balance out the scone. *This*, she thought, *is how a morning should start*.

She looked at the shelf behind her, a display organized by the bookshop next door, and decided to add a book to her morning. After a little perusal, she found a romantic comedy set in London and decided it would be the perfect accompaniment to her coffee and scone. She delved into the story.

"Good morning." A deep voice startled her out of the world she'd escaped to.

"Oh my stars." Krisi set her book down and put a hand over her jumping heart. Her brain felt like she was coming out of a fog.

Brian, the man she'd met at the farmers' market, stood in front of her, grinning, and dang if he didn't look even better in dress slacks than jeans.

"Brian?" Krisi couldn't believe *Brian* was standing in front of her.

The corners of his green eyes crinkled. "Melody said the new resident was here, but I had no idea it was you."

"*You're* the manager?" Disappointment lodged in her stomach as she pieced things together. In the first instant she'd recognized him, she thought, hoped, he was a resident at The Athenian and was looking forward to getting to know him better. But now...

Brian grinned. "It's one of my titles. I do whatever needs to be done around here."

Krisi looked around the café, stunned to see how full it had become. How had she not heard all these people come in? She looked at the book and was surprised to see she was already a quarter of the way through it.

Looking back up at Brian, she waved a hand to the seat across from her. "You're welcome to join me, if you'd like."

"So how was your first night here?" he asked, settling himself in the chair.

"It was good but too short." She laughed. "I forgot to close my drapes last night, so I was woken up by the sunrise. Something I haven't experienced in years."

He chuckled. "It was a good one this morning, wasn't it?"

"You saw it too?"

"I watch the sunrise from the rooftop most mornings."

"From the roof? That must be a spectacular place to watch."

"It's a good way to start the day." He paused for a moment and took a sip of coffee. "You're welcome to join me, if you'd like."

She looked at him, his green eyes piercing her. While a romantic relationship with him was out of the question—her father would have a coronary if she brought an apartment manager home to meet him. Hardly what he'd consider an *advantageous partner*. But she could use a friend, and he'd certainly been one to her at the market.

"I'd love to watch the sunrise from the roof with you. Tell me what time and I'll be there."

Brian's eyebrows shot up. "I'll meet you at the sixth floor elevators at five o'clock tomorrow morning. That work for you?"

"Absolutely." She wasn't going to let him know she never got up at five in the morning, but this would help with the new morning routine she wanted to start.

He grinned at her. "I'll bring coffee, and you might want a blanket. It's still pretty chilly in the morning." He picked up his mug and stood. "Welcome to The Athenian, Krisi. Glad you're here."

She watched him walk away, stopping to chat at almost every table on his way out. For a moment, Krisi indulged herself, appreciating his departing figure. A subtle pull, an undeniable attraction tugged her senses, even knowing he wasn't the man for her. She couldn't deny herself the simple pleasure of watching him walk away.

Brian's silhouette commanded attention, his figure imposing yet graceful. Her gaze traced the line of his shoulders, broad and confident, tapering to a slender waist. Her mind wandered back to their motorcycle ride, when her arms had been laced around his slim waist. His black slacks looked tailor-made and accentuated his physique with a subtle elegance.

"He's a good-looking one, isn't he?"

Krisi startled and found Melody standing next to her table, also watching Brian. She grinned at being caught. "That he is, Melody. He seems to know everyone."

"He does. Even the regular patrons who don't live in the building, he's made a point to get to know them." Melody turned and looked at Krisi. Her eyes narrowed, just a bit. "He's a good guy."

Krisi nodded. She recognized and acknowledged the warning—don't mess with Brian. Well, that wasn't going to be a problem. She was only looking for a friend. Even if her hammering pulse told a different story. She looked at her thin silver watch.

"Oh my stars. I can't believe it's eight thirty already." She looked at the book in her hand. "Can I put this on my tab too?"

At Melody's nod, she grabbed her purse and the book, and with a quick goodbye to Melody, she headed out the door. Running down the corridor past the bookshop and the spa, Krisi arrived at the elevator to find Nikki waiting.

"Krisi, my goodness...you're up? Is everything okay?"

Krisi grinned. "I'm glad I caught you before you found my bed empty."

The elevator doors opened and they stepped inside. Nikki pushed the button for the sixth floor before turning to her friend.

"What in the world are you doing awake so early?"

"I'm an early bird, Nikki. You should know that by now," Krisi deadpanned.

Nikki gave her a bland look and arched an eyebrow. Waiting.

"Ha, okay. I forgot to close my curtains last night. I've been up for hours. I watched the sunrise, had a cup of coffee at Melody's—which by the way, she has the most delicious coffee and pastries."

The elevator doors opened again, and they stepped into the hallway in front of the apartment. Krisi, realizing she hadn't grabbed her keys on the way out, stepped back and waited for Nikki to unlock the door. She made a mental note to put her key by the door.

"Well, it sounds like I don't need to make breakfast or—" Nikki's stopped speaking midsentence as they stepped into the living room.

"Daddy?" Krisi was shocked to see her father sitting on the couch in her living room.

He looked at Nikki. "Go make a pot of coffee." It wasn't a question, but a demand. Fortunately, Nikki was used to her father's terse manner, not that it excused his rude behavior.

"She's not a maid, Daddy."

Ignoring the comment, he waited for Nikki to leave the room, then turned to Krisi with a look of disgust on his face. "And you? Whose bed did you just crawl out of?"

Taken aback by his blunt and crude question, Krisi took her time sitting in the chair across from him. She straightened her spine. "Not that it's any of your business, but I didn't crawl out of anyone's bed. I slept here, by myself, last night. How did you get into my apartment?"

"Don't talk to me like that." His eyes narrowed at her tone. "Whether you're under my roof or not, everything you do is my business. Everything you do reflects on me and the family."

Her stiff spine wavered under his harsh tone. She noticed he'd deftly ignored her question. It bothered her—a lot—that he'd been able to get in when she wasn't home. His comment about his business made her wonder what, exactly, he wanted from her. She hadn't recently been linked to anyone in the gossip magazines, so she had no idea where he was going with this.

"What can I do for you this morning?" She knew her smile didn't reach her eyes, but it was the best she could muster in the moment.

Nikki came in with a tray holding a coffee pot, two mugs, and the creamer Krisi liked.

Her father looked at her. "We're having a private discussion, if you don't mind."

"Not at all, Mr. St. Claire. I wanted to bring you the coffee you asked for." Nikki turned, gave Krisi a very subtle wink, and walked out of the room.

"She's much too comfortable around here. Too big for her britches, if you ask me."

"Then I guess it's a good thing she works for me, not you," Krisi said blandly.

He turned back to her. "I've set up a lunch for you and Senator Black next week. Tuesday at noon." He rattled off the name of a trendy restaurant near the state capitol building.

Krisi paused. "Now you're in charge of my social calendar?"

"I told you I want you to get to know him. This is an opportunity to do so."

With that, he stood and walked out the door. Krisi would have laughed at the absurdity of their conversation, except she knew he firmly believed he *could* control her. And while she could just *not* show up for the lunch, she wasn't sure if it was worth it.

She was shocked her future was being planned without her consent or input, and she had no idea what to do about it. She thought of Brian and knew what her father would think of even just a friendship with him. He would think Brian unworthy of a St. Claire heir.

But the big question in her mind was what did *she* believe? Did it matter whether Brian was *worthy* or not?

Chapter 6

BRIAN

EARLY MONDAY MORNING, BRIAN stood outside the elevator on the sixth floor waiting for Krisi. He hadn't exactly snuck out of his apartment, but at the same time, he hadn't invited his sister to join him like he usually would. It had probably been a mistake to invite Krisi. He'd never invited a resident—well, except Marilyn—to join him for sunrise on the rooftop. The people who lived in the building were rich; Krisi was a whole different level of rich. Way out of his league.

But it was hard to forget how much he'd enjoyed her company at the farmers' market.

Hopefully, she was just as real now that he knew who she really was.

Kristine St. Claire.

He wondered why she'd lied about visiting a friend when he dropped her off. He turned when he heard a door open down the hall and saw Krisi walking toward him. He grinned at the slippers on her feet. Granted, they were sparkly and furry, but maybe she was as down-to-earth as he'd originally thought. Seeing something tucked under her arm, he realized she'd taken his recommendation of bringing a blanket to heart.

She grinned, eyeing the coffee in his hand. "Not sure why the early bird would want a worm. Coffee seems more civilized."

"I wasn't sure you would show," he said with a raised eyebrow. "This is much earlier than most folks around here get up."

"Ha...well, I can admit waking up to see the sunrise yesterday was a fluke."

She stepped into the elevator behind him. He tapped a plastic card on the control panel, then pushed a button labeled RT.

"But today was on purpose. Thank you for the invite and for bringing coffee."

The elevator stopped, and Krisi followed him onto the rooftop. It was, as expected, a chilly, windy morning. She'd be glad she brought a blanket. He led her to the private space he'd set up with a hightop table and two stools next to the wall at the edge of the roof. He placed the two coffees on the table, then pulled out a stool for her.

"I asked Melody how you took your coffee, so hopefully this is okay." He handed her an insulated mug, then sat on the other stool. Melody had been wary about him getting cozy with Krisi but told him she liked chocolate, so he'd bought a mocha flavored creamer and laced her coffee with it.

Krisi took a sip of the hot liquid. "Oh my." She looked at him. "I don't know what magic you put in here, but this is divine. I could wake up to this every morning." Her eyes went wide, and she quickly turned away to look at the skyline around them. "This is an amazing view. Wait..." She looked at him again, her eyebrows knitting together. "This is the same view from my balcony, just higher up. It was you—well, your coffee, I smelled yesterday."

He grinned at her. "I don't usually have to worry about anyone else being awake at this hour."

"I was dying for a cup of coffee but wanted to watch the sunrise. It was a struggle smelling yours." She laughed.

He watched her pull the blanket around her shoulders and push her long blond hair away from her face. She was beautiful.

"I appreciate that you didn't worry about putting on makeup or doing your hair." Her hand immediately went to her hair. "No, you look great." He'd never been smooth, but he was really fumbling this morning. "I just...I hoped you would come as you are. I come up before I shower, so I'm usually in sweats and a hoodie."

She lowered her hand from her hair and picked up her coffee. "So do you live here?"

This was always an awkward question, and most residents didn't ask. "I do. On the second floor." He could have lied, but it was easier to be up front and honest with her. Keeping track of lies had never appealed to him. Not that he expected more than friendship.

If that were true, he wondered why he'd invited her up here in the first place. When he invited Marilyn to join him, they'd already been friends. She'd never accepted his offer to get up at the crack of dawn, as she called it.

He watched Krisi mull that piece of information over and wondered what was going through her head.

He refocused on the horizon, and it immediately captured his attention. She looked at him, and he nodded toward the sun peeking through the clouds. He heard her gasp as the sky morphed into glorious colors before their eyes.

They sat silently watching the sky and drinking coffee. Brian had never shared this experience with anyone other than his sister. It was interesting. Intimate, almost. Her eyes were wide with wonder as she watched the show in the eastern sky.

After several minutes, she looked over at him again, her eyes sparkling in the early morning light. "You watch this *every* morning?"

"Well, only mornings that aren't rainy or snowy."

"It's a beautiful way to start the day. Thanks for sharing it with me." She gave him a contented smile, then returned her gaze to the sky.

They watched in silence until the sun was fully above the horizon.

She turned to him again. Opened her mouth to speak, closed it. Then started again. "Melody said if I need anything, I should come to you."

"Absolutely. What can I help you with?" His curiosity was piqued with her sudden change of mood. Her face had gone from relaxed to tense in the space of her question.

She set her coffee on the table and laced her fingers together. "What could I do to stop someone from coming into my apartment uninvited?"

Brian sat up straighter. "Someone entered your apartment?"

She nodded. "After coffee yesterday, I went back up to my apartment to find my father there. I don't know how he got in, but I don't want him to have access to my home."

He narrowed his eyes, thinking about what she'd said. "I assume neither you nor Nikki gave him a key?"

She shook her head. "No. I certainly didn't give him a key, and I know Nikki wouldn't have."

"I can arrange to have the lock changed today, if you'd like."

"Yes." She paused for a minute, thinking, then nodded. "Yes, I'd like the lock changed. Thank you."

"I'll give you a call later with the details, but it'll be done today."

Mr. St. Claire, tech billionaire and local philanthropist, had broken into his daughter's apartment? What in the world was going on?

Brian's carefully crafted, orderly world was shifting, and he wasn't sure what to think of it.

Brian quietly let himself back into his apartment, trying not to wake his sister, only to find her standing in the living room, her hand on one hip. *So much for sneaking in*, he thought.

Shelby narrowed her eyes. "Who did you watch the sunrise with? Because it certainly wasn't me."

"Mornin'. I wasn't sure if you wanted to be woken up this morning," he said, dodging her question.

"It was the new renter, wasn't it?"

Man, she was scary sometimes. "Why do you think I watched the sunrise with anyone?"

She laughed, her tone more relaxed. "What's her name? I can't wait to meet her."

He shook his head and walked into the kitchen. The fact that his sister was going into marketing instead of detective work was a shame. He poured himself another cup of coffee and turned to look at her, holding up the pot. At her nod, he refilled her cup, then sat at the dining table with her.

"Her name is Krisi. Yes, she's the new tenant, and—"

"I knew it," Shelby crowed triumphantly.

"*And,*" he continued, "she's just a friend."

"If that were true, you would have woken me up this morning." Before he could object, she continued, "Though I have to say, I'm completely disappointed the new renter isn't a hot young billionaire *guy*."

Brian rolled his eyes and shook his head.

"So what's on the docket today?" Shelby asked. "I was thinking of hitting up Graham for a job this summer."

"Graham? Nashville Uncorked Graham? But...that's a wine bar." It didn't matter that his sister was twenty-two, he was unprepared for her to work in a bar.

"I know it's a wine bar, silly. I want to learn about wine, and I think he's the best person around here to teach me. Next summer, I want to do an internship at a winery, so I need to learn about wine now."

"Huh." Brian was impressed by her logic, even if he didn't like the idea of his little sister working in a bar. "Why wine? You've never had any interest before...at least, not that I've seen." Her degree would be in marketing, but he'd never really thought about what she would do with it.

"In one of my classes, we had to prepare a marketing campaign in a randomly picked market. Mine was wine. I visited different wineries in Indiana and became hooked. I'd really like to spend some time at a vineyard, so that's my goal for next summer."

When the heck did his little sister grow up and start making adult plans? He'd kinda hoped she'd want to work with him at The Athenian.

"Napa Valley?" he asked.

"Well, Napa would certainly be nice, but I'd really like to spend the summer in Italy."

"Italy?" His voice cracked. Shelby had never been that far away. And to be gone for the whole summer, the only time he had to spend with her...it would be hard.

She put her hand on his. "It's okay, Brian. You have a whole year to get used to the idea."

Life was shifting faster than he was comfortable with. He and Shelby had been a unit since their parents died. It had been hard when she left for college, but at least she was only four hours away. He knew he'd eventually have to let Shelby go, but it felt like it was coming too quickly. He couldn't—no, wouldn't—hold her back from her dreams.

But Italy?!

Early Tuesday, Brian and Shelby left the apartment to catch the sunrise on the roof. Brian wanted to invite Krisi again but wasn't sure how that would go with Shelby.

"I always forget how early the sun comes up in summer," Shelby grumbled. Her blond hair was poking out from under a beanie she'd shoved over her head. She wore a canary yellow terry cloth robe with flannel pajamas and carried a blanket in one hand and an insulated mug of coffee in the other.

Brian reached out and tousled her hat. "And you complained yesterday about not being woken up."

Shelby reached the elevator first and punched the up button with her elbow. She took a step back in surprise when the doors immediately opened to reveal Krisi was standing behind them. She also had a blanket over one arm and an insulated mug of what he assumed was coffee in her other hand.

Krisi looked from Brian to Shelby. "Oh!" She took a step back, seeming uncomfortable.

Brian stepped forward. "Krisi, it's good to see you." He joined her in the elevator and turned to wait for Shelby. "I was hoping you'd join us this morning."

She looked at him again, then back to Shelby. Recognizing what was probably going through her mind, he said, "I'd like you to meet my sister, Shelby." He turned to his sister. "Shelby, this is our newest resident, Krisi."

Both women immediately smiled.

"It's a pleasure to meet you, Shelby. I know you just got back to Nashville, so I won't join you if you want to hang out with your brother alone."

"No, of course not. It's great to meet you, Krisi. Brian didn't mention you were Kristine St. Claire though. I probably would have brushed my hair if I'd known." She grinned at Krisi's slippers and velour robe. "I'm glad to see you got the dress code memo."

Brian shook his head and pushed the button for the roof before leaning against the wall. "How's the new lock working out?"

He'd reached out to a locksmith friend and was able to get him in quickly. When they'd learned that Krisi's lock had been tampered with, he installed a new electronic lock that couldn't be picked.

"It's great, thank you. I appreciate you getting it taken care of so quickly."

"Not a problem."

Shelby, he noticed, was silently watching the two of them. If he had to guess, she was creating a scenario in her head that wasn't even close to reality. Kristine St. Claire was out of his league. And from what he'd seen in the papers, she went through men like a sommelier sampling wine. Her palate was refined, her options vast, but no one lasted.

The doors quietly slid open, and they stepped onto the dark rooftop. "Go ahead and take the stools, you two." He only had two stools here; there'd never been a need for more. Shelby set his coffee on the table between the two of them, so he stood in the middle. He made a mental note to bring up another stool.

"Oh, Brian, take this stool." Krisi made to stand up, but he laid his hand on her shoulder and kept her in her seat.

"No, I'm good. You keep the stool."

"Well...thank you." She took a sip of coffee and gave a little shudder. "I need to know what creamer you used yesterday. This isn't nearly as good as what you made."

"I'll be happy to share it with you." Brian laughed.

"He does make good coffee, doesn't he?" Shelby took a sip of her own, then set it on the table.

They sat in comfortable silence, watching the sky for a few minutes. Both women were wrapped up in blankets, sipping coffee and watching the ever-changing sky in front of them. Brian stood between them, leaning his elbows on the table. Not the most comfortable way to watch the sunrise, but he was pleased to be here with both Shelby and Krisi.

"So, Krisi, how do you like The Athenian?" Shelby asked.

"Beyond having lock issues, I really like it here. I haven't checked out the shops downstairs...well, other than the coffee shop. Melody makes an amazing cup of coffee too."

"OMG," Shelby said. "Have you tried the Music City Mocha? It's to die for."

"That's exactly what I had." Krisi laughed. "It *is* to die for."

The sun started peeking over the horizon, capturing their attention again. Brian took another sip of coffee, his gaze going back and forth from the horizon to Krisi. He was glad she was wearing comfortable clothes and slippers. Though he did notice her slippers were warmer and more functional than the stylish ones she'd worn the morning before. It had delighted him to see her in the elevator, knowing she wanted to watch the sunrise again.

With *him*.

"You need to check out Uncorked. If you like wine, which I imagine you do, you'll really like his selection." Shelby looked at Krisi

"Why do you imagine she likes wine?" Brian asked.

"Well, she's rich. And from my experience, rich people like wine," Shelby stated bluntly.

"Shelby!" Brian closed his eyes and shook his head. Sometimes his sister was mortifying. He looked at Krisi, only to find her laughing.

"Oh, she's fine," Krisi said. "I *am* rich." She shrugged. "My father just cut me off from the family funds because I moved in here. I suspect he thinks I won't last long on my own."

Shelby narrowed her eyes. "But you've got your perfume company, right?"

Brian was confused. "What perfume company?"

Shelby looked at Brian. "You don't think she just promotes perfume for others, do you? Never mind, you're never on social media so you don't even know what I'm talking about." She turned back to Krisi. "It *is* yours, right?"

"Um, wow. Yes, it's my company, but no one knows. Not even my family. Or maybe especially my family."

"What perfume company?" Brian asked again. How did his little sister know this when no one else did?

"Scent SCK," Shelby and Krisi said at the same time.

Krisi looked at Shelby. "How'd you figure it out?"

"Well, it wouldn't make sense to continually promote the same company over the years just for a small percentage. And SCK...St. Claire, Kristine."

She looked at Krisi and Brian, like it was obvious and everyone should have made the connection.

Krisi stared at her for a full ten seconds before bursting out laughing. "Let me know if you ever want a job. I could use someone smart and clever on my marketing team."

Brian sat back and thought about what he'd just learned. Krisi had created and ran a perfume company. He was having a hard time wrapping his brain around what he thought he knew about her—granted it was from newspapers—with what he was learning about her from his experience. She wasn't a shallow socialite without depth. Not only was she creative, but she was a smart businessperson. He respected that.

And maybe if he was wrong about this, he might be wrong about her relationships with men. Something to think about.

Chapter 7

KRISI

Three wishes:

- *More sunrises on the roof.*

- *Get through lunch with senator.*

- *Learn more about Brian.*

TUESDAY MORNING, AFTER WATCHING
the sunrise with Brian and Shelby, Krisi

stood in her bedroom with Nikki, contemplating what to wear to the dreaded lunch with Senator Black. Krisi didn't keep up with local politics, and she pictured a stodgy old man. He'd probably been in politics since before Krisi was born.

"Pick out the most boring outfit I've got." She sighed, resigned to her fate.

Nikki laughed. "It's just lunch, Krisi. Besides, he might be nice."

Krisi rolled her eyes at her friend. "Just grab something unappealing, and let's get this over with."

Nikki disappeared into the closet and came out a few minutes later with a pair of black slacks, a high-neck black sleeveless sweater, and a red-and-black jacket. "Mournful enough?"

Krisi couldn't help but laugh. "I know, I know. I'm being overly dramatic. But I *really* don't like Daddy trying to control my life."

"Then don't go to lunch with the senator. It would send a message to your father, and with the new lock, he won't be able to get back in to give you grief about it."

Krisi paused on her way to the bathroom. "Don't go?" The thought of defying her father's orders both appealed to and terrified her. She let out a long breath. "I'm not sure I'm ready for that, but I will let the good senator know my father is not in control of my social calendar."

As she changed into the outfit Nikki had chosen, she thought about the lock. Brian had put on a new electronic lock that needed a key fob to open. Only she, Nikki, and Brian had fobs. Her suspicion that her father had someone pick her lock had been confirmed. It was staggering to think he thought that was okay. He would be angry when he discovered the change. A small step of defiance. Maybe not as blatant as not going to this lunch, but still, her father would certainly recognize he wasn't welcome if he tried to gain access to her apartment again.

Stepping out of the bathroom, she looked in the mirror. "So what do you think?"

"As always, you look lovely."

Krisi frowned. "As long as it doesn't suggest I'm interested in anything more than lunch with the man."

"Since the only skin visible is on your hands, I think you're safe." Nikki grinned. "On a different note, I'm going to spend some time answering the emails that have been piling up over the last couple of days. Have you given any thought to setting up retail space in Nashville?"

Krisi sat on the chaise longue to pull on her boots. "We currently have shops in London, Paris, Madrid, and New York. Nashville's not the next logical spot, but it does make sense since it's where I am."

"You ready to be outed?"

"With Daddy officially cutting me off, I have a feeling it'll happen whether I'm ready or not." She stood, touched up her lipstick, and made her way out of the bedroom. "I think I'll ask Brian about retail space downtown. That'll at least give us some information on whether it's a good path to follow. I'll be back in a couple of hours."

"Brian's name seems to be popping up a lot lately..."

Krisi rolled her eyes. "He's a wealth of knowledge and incredibly helpful." She wasn't going to mention that she thought he was also very attractive.

With a heaviness in the pit of her stomach at the thought of lunch, Krisi headed out the door. It would be fine, she told herself. She knew how to lunch with movers and shakers. After all, it's what she'd been bred to do. Senator Michael Black was just another colleague of her father's. Usually, she was given an agenda, or at least topics to bring up or steer clear of. This time, she'd been given nothing.

The doors of the elevator opened into the lobby, and she saw Brian sitting in his office just off the lobby. She decided it was as good a time as any to ask about retail space. And he was a pleasant diversion.

She stood outside his door and studied him. He was wearing glasses, which she hadn't seen before. They did nothing to detract from his looks. If anything, they made him even more handsome. He was working intently at his computer, a slight frown on his face.

"Knock, knock."

He startled as he looked up. "Oh, Krisi, I didn't hear you."

"You looked pretty engrossed. Sorry to bother you. I just have a quick question."

"Sure, what can I help with?"

His smile warmed her through. He was such a nice, genuine person.

"I'm wondering if you can recommend where I might look for retail space downtown. I need somewhere that screams high-end but isn't too big."

"I just happen to know the perfect place." He laughed. "That's actually what I was working on before you poked your head in. The art gallery in the lobby"—he pointed to the dark business—"didn't renew their contract, so I need to find a new business partner for that space. I'm happy to show it to you, if you'd like."

"Here? At The Athenian? Oh my stars, how perfect." She looked at her watch. "Shoot,

I don't have time now, but maybe this afternoon?"

"I'll be around," he said with a smile. "Just let me know when's a good time."

After a quick goodbye, Krisi found her car in the garage, and twenty minutes later, she walked into the restaurant for the dreaded lunch with Senator Black. In her mind, she was early at only five minutes late. It didn't count as late until you hit ten minutes. The hostess led her through the dimly lit room to a table in the back. A dark-haired man faced away from her, so it wasn't until she was next to him that she could see her lunch date was not only younger than expected but handsome as well.

As soon as she stepped up to the table, he stood and took her hand in his. "Kristine, a pleasure to finally meet you." He dropped her hand and pulled out the chair across from his before sitting back down. "You are even more attractive than your pictures."

"Thank you, Senator." She knew how to play the game. Surprisingly, his dark eyes didn't stray down her body, instead staying intensely on hers. The man in front of her was, no doubt, what her father had in mind when he said he wanted her to choose an *advantageous* partner. Her stomach churned just thinking about it.

"Can I order you a glass of wine?" He already had a glass in front of him, and he put his hand up to call the waiter.

"No, but thank you. I have to drive home and have a full schedule this afternoon, so drinking at lunch probably isn't a good idea." She knew it was bad manners to not join your lunch date in a drink, especially if they already had one, but she wasn't overly concerned with manners, and she certainly wasn't interested in pleasing this man. He might be a handsome surprise, but he was old enough to be her father.

He nodded at her comment. "No problem. What can Carlo bring you to drink instead?" The waiter had just arrived and stood waiting.

"I'll just have some water, please," she said to the man. "Sparkling with lime." She knew it was expected for her to be fussy. The waiter smiled at her with a little nod and turned away from the table. She was so sick of expectations.

Her thoughts wandered to Brian, to the fact that he didn't have any expectations when it came to her. She didn't have to act a certain way or look a certain way. It was refreshing. It amazed her how relaxed she'd been during the sunrises she spent with him.

"Thank you for having lunch with me today," the senator said. "I apologize for going through your father to make the date."

"I'm not a fan of having someone else in charge of my calendar. Especially my father." While she didn't yet know the reason for her attendance at this lunch, she didn't like her father's maneuvering of her time.

"Next time, I'll make sure to go directly to you," he said. His white teeth stood out when he smiled, as did a small dimple to the left of his mouth.

She thought of Brian's smile, a little off-center. And the small gap between his front teeth made it not perfect. Yet somehow it was.

"Presumptuous," she said with a raised eyebrow. She picked up the menu and looked it over. She wasn't hungry and had no desire to dine with this man, but etiquette dictated she order something. After thirty-plus years of having manners and etiquette hammered into her, she realized now how much she did on autopilot, just because it was expected. It was something she'd need to change. She was fine with manners, but she realized she needed to put some boundaries in place.

Feeling the senator's eyes still on her, she looked at him.

"I get the feeling you don't want to be here." A rather direct comment for this stage of their acquaintance.

"I wasn't given an option, Senator. I was told to be here, so I am here. Maybe *you* can tell me why?"

His eyes widened at her comment, though she wasn't completely convinced his surprise was genuine. Her outspoken tone was probably a surprise.

"My apologies." He paused, as if gathering his thoughts. "I asked your father to extend this invitation to have lunch with me. I'm sorry it came across as a demand."

She nodded but didn't say anything.

"I really just wanted to get to know you. I've worked with your father for several years, and he mentioned you'd moved back to Nashville. I was hoping to make you feel welcome."

"Well, thank you. That was thoughtful of you. Unnecessary, but thoughtful." She leaned back in her chair and worked to relax her shoulders. He was an attractive man with impeccable manners, so she may as well try to relax and get through lunch. There was still something she didn't understand. *Why* was it so important to her father that she have lunch with this man?

They placed their orders and relaxed into superficial conversation. They knew a lot of the same people, so it was easy to catch up on who was doing what with whom. He seemed to have his finger on the pulse of everything. She imagined his impression of her was one of a spoiled heiress who aimlessly flitted around the world. She was comfortable letting him think that and kept the conversation surface-level.

Her thoughts again wandered to Brian. Their conversations weren't superficial. He asked her challenging questions and actually listened to the answers. At least, it felt like he did. He'd been surprised and pleased to hear she was a businesswoman. If she were really being honest, she was attracted to him, and she liked how he made her feel.

Their meals came, and Krisi sipped her soup. Her food was delicious, so lunch wasn't a complete bust.

"You surprise me," Black commented and waved his fork toward her soup bowl. "I'm not sure I've ever had lunch with a woman who didn't order a salad."

It took everything in her not to roll her eyes. "Hmm," she hummed evasively. Growing up, her father had almost always commented on what her mother ate. And as Krisi had grown older, he'd made a few comments to her as well. Like it was a crime to enjoy food. She was careful with what she ate—health was important to her—but she didn't deny herself what she wanted anymore.

"I certainly hope it doesn't make you uncomfortable that I enjoy eating something other than salad," she said innocently...well, sarcastically, but she tried to make it come across as innocent.

A slight frown flitted across his face. "No, of course not. It's refreshing to meet a woman who isn't obsessed with her figure."

Not interested in continuing *that* conversation, Krisi asked him about the bills he'd been working on. As expected, he spent the rest of their meal talking about himself and his job. After listening to him for an hour, she glanced at her watch. She'd made an art of acting like she was trying to be discrete but failing.

"Oh my stars, Senator." She exaggerated her southern accent. "I can't believe how late it is." She'd finished her soup a good thirty minutes earlier, and the senator had gone through two glasses of wine but only half of his meal since he'd been talking so much. She carefully folded her napkin and pushed her chair away from the table. "I apologize, but I have another commitment."

Startled by her sudden departure, the senator stood and leaned in to kiss her cheeks. Krisi stuck out her hand, taking him off guard and leaving him in an awkward position. He smoothly pulled back from her and shook her hand.

"Thank you for lunch, Senator," she said, then started to walk away.

"I'd love to do this again," Senator Black said quickly.

She turned her head to look at him. "Make sure you don't go through my father."

With a small smile, knowing she hadn't given him any way to contact her directly, she continued out the door and to her car. She could now understand Lily's comment about him giving her the creeps. While everything on the surface was exactly as it should be—he was handsome, well-dressed, had respectable manners—it felt to her there was much more under the surface. If she dug just a little, she doubted she would like what she found.

Later that evening, Krisi stepped out of the elevator and made her way to the wine bar on the first floor to meet her brother for a drink. She'd been pleased to get the text saying he wanted to see her new place.

The afternoon had been filled with viewing the retail space in the lobby—which she loved—going through her calendar with Nikki, responding to emails that needed her personal touch, then changing for drinks with her brother.

She couldn't remember the last time she and Alex had drinks together. Probably the previous year when he visited her in Paris. At only a year apart, they'd grown up as best friends. Even through boarding school, they kept an eye out for each other. After she moved overseas, they hadn't spent as much time together. These days, Alex worked a lot, trying to prove to their father he was worthy to take over the business.

Hurrying through the door, she spotted Alex at the bar and rushed over to him. He hated when she was late. And she was always late, according to him.

"I know, I know. I'm late." She laughed as she kissed his cheek.

He took her hands and held her at arm's length to check her over. "You're looking good, sis." He grinned at her. "I like that color on you. Looks great!"

She grinned at his comment about her lime-green pantsuit. Alex was even more of a fashion diva than she was and always remarked on her clothes. She strived to wear clothes worthy of his scrutiny whenever they got together. "And you." She looked at his black-and-teal plaid slacks and teal button-down shirt. She tugged his colorful tie. "You're looking sharp, as always."

"Got a reputation to maintain." He laughed while straightening his tie.

Krisi climbed onto the stool next to him and waved to the bartender.

"Evenin', ma'am, what can I get you?"

She ordered a merlot. This was her first time in Uncorked, but she already loved its vibe. Rich colors, leather seats, and modern lighting made for a fun atmosphere.

Within a couple of minutes, the bartender came back with her wine and slid it in front of her. "My name's Beau. If you need anything else, just holler."

Krisi picked up her glass and nodded. "Will do, thanks."

"So how's the new digs?" Alex asked, looking around the bar.

"My apartment is wonderful. Spacious, open, perfect for me."

"How'd Mother and Father take you moving out?"

"Mother, as always, didn't have a lot to say. I don't think she cares if I'm there or not. Father, on the other hand, was furious."

"Really? Why?"

She paused, debating how much to share. Alex was close with their father. They worked together every day, and she didn't want to ruin their relationship.

"Go ahead," he said. "Just say it."

"Father showed up in my apartment."

"What do you mean, *in* your apartment?

"He was sitting in my apartment when Nikki and I walked in."

"But..." Alex looked at her, confused. "You gave him a key?"

She shook her head. "He had someone pick the lock." She watched Alex's eyes go wide. "I had the lock changed, but yeah..."

Alex took a drink of his beer. "So after all that, what did he want?"

"He'd arranged a lunch date for me. With Senator Black. He made it clear it wasn't optional, that I needed to rearrange my schedule to make this date."

"Senator Black?" Alex twisted his pint glass, his brow furrowed. "Why would he want you to have lunch with Black? It doesn't make sense. I don't even think Father *likes* Senator Black. Why is it important for you to have lunch with him?"

Krisi shrugged. "I don't know."

"Have you had lunch with him yet?"

"Yeah, today." Krisi rolled her eyes. "Lily said the senator gave her the creeps. After spending time with him, I have to agree with her." Alex lifted an eyebrow, and she continued, "He presents well. You know, he's attractive, has a good job, good manners, but there's something off. I could tell he was holding back, but I'm not sure what. Or what exactly it even means."

Alex leaned back in his chair, looking thoughtful. "I know the senator just passed a bill that's extremely beneficial to our company. I wonder what Father promised to get it passed?"

Krisi could feel her eyes go wide and her stomach churn. "Daddy wouldn't..."

She stopped midsentence. She wasn't convinced he *wouldn't*. Her father had changed in the years she'd been abroad. She wasn't sure she even knew who he was anymore.

"We don't know anything for sure," Alex said quickly. "I'll do some feeling out with Father this week to see if I can learn anything."

"Hey, Krisi" Shelby stood with an empty tray in her hand and wore a black apron with pockets.

"Oh hi, Shelby." She hadn't seen Shelby come up to them. She looked around and saw Brian at the back of the room, near the entrance, and gave him a smile. She wanted to introduce him to her brother. "How's the job going?"

Shelby grinned. "I'm loving it." She looked at Alex. "Hi, I'm Shelby."

Krisi laughed. "Sorry. This is my brother, Alex. Alex, meet Shelby. Shelby, her brother, and I have been watching the sunrise together."

Alex arched his eyebrow again. He knew she wasn't an early riser. "Good to meet you, Shelby. What'd you do to get Krisi out of bed so early?"

Shelby grinned at him. "I think it's more what my *brother* did that got her up early."

Interest piqued, Alex questioned Shelby. "And who is your brother?"

Krisi could feel her cheeks warm. She wanted to look at Brian but knew her brother wouldn't miss it and would tease her mercilessly.

"Brian," Shelby answered. "He kind of does everything around here." She looked up and caught the bartender's eye. "Oh, gotta go. Have a good night, y'all."

"Brian?" Alex said as soon as Shelby was gone. "An apartment building manager?"

"He's a good guy, Alex."

"Just to be clear," Alex said, looking into her eyes. "I'm not judging. But I'm pretty sure you know who *will* have a problem with it. Especially if *his* plans include a certain senator."

Krisi nodded. "I know." She let out a sigh. Not feeling like hanging around the bar anymore, Krisi stood. "Want to see my apartment?"

Alex dropped a fifty on the bar and followed her. Disappointment settled deep in her heart when she realized Brian was no longer at the corner table. She'd really wanted to see him. Talk to him. Introduce Alex to him.

She'd really wanted Alex's impressions of the man who had captured so many of her thoughts.

Chapter 8

BRIAN

FRIDAY EVENING, BRIAN WAS sitting in Uncorked with a glass of red wine when Krisi breezed through the doorway. In the short time they'd known each other, he'd only seen her in the velour warm-up suits she wore to watch the sunrise and her luncheon attire. Tonight, she looked like the heir she was. She wore a pair of green pants, somewhere between lime and avocado, a pale pink tube top, and a jacket the same color as her pants. Her shoes were towering and matched the pale pink purse swinging from her shoulder. Her head was held high, her long blond hair straight down her back, and a diamond choker around her neck sparkled with each step.

He stood, preparing to greet her, but she rushed past him to join a man at the bar. She kissed him on both cheeks, playfully tugged on his tie, then sat on a stool next to him. She leaned into him, laughing at whatever he'd said. It was obvious they had a personal relationship.

"You might want to tone down the lasers coming from your eyes."

He looked up to see Shelby standing in front of him with a tray in her hand.

"What?"

"You looked like you were trying to drill a hole through someone with your eyes." She glanced over her should to where he'd been staring. "Ah, Krisi's here and sitting with someone else. I see. Good-looking, isn't he?"

He glared at her, annoyed she'd caught him staring like a lovesick puppy.

"You want some more wine?" Shelby asked. It was her second day on the job, and Brian had stopped by to see how it was going. Krisi's arrival had thrown him off his primary mission of keeping an eye on his baby sister. Shelby, he was learning, could handle herself. And she was good at her job. She seemed to already know a lot about wine and was personable with the clientele.

"No, I'll finish this, then take off. How's the new bartender? Beau is it?

"Beau's great." Shelby turned to look at the man behind the bar. "He's a good-looking one too."

Brain looked at the man. Tall, tanned, blond-streaked brown hair. He shrugged. *Great. Another good-looking guy.* "Don't go getting any ideas. He's much too old for you."

Shelby laughed. "I gotta go, but I'll see you later."

He watched her make her way through the tables, checking at each one, taking orders, picking up empties, moving on. When she got to the bar, she emptied her tray and made her way to Krisi. He saw them give each other a hug, and it looked like Krisi introduced Shelby to her date. Krisi turned to look right at Brian and smiled.

Dang it, she'd caught him staring. As soon as she turned back to her date, Brian stood and threw a twenty on the table for his sister's tip, then headed out the door. He didn't want to watch the woman he'd grown interested in enjoy a date with another man. That was just torture.

He unlocked then relocked his office door behind him before crossing to the back stairs and going up to the second floor. He let himself into his apartment, grabbed a beer from the fridge, and threw himself on the couch. He stood up again without even taking a drink and paced the living room, then decided he needed fresh air. He grabbed a hoodie, picked up his beer from the coffee table, and was out the door, heading for the elevator. When the doors opened, he was shocked to see Krisi and her date in the elevator, laughing.

"Oh, Brian," Krisi exclaimed, her eyes sparkling. "I wanted to intro—"

Brian turned on his heel. "Excuse me, I forgot something," he called over his shoulder.

As soon as he heard the doors close again, he made his way back to the elevator and punched the button. When the doors opened several minutes later, the elevator was empty, but Krisi's citrusy scent lingered, as if to torture him. He pushed the button for the rooftop and leaned against the wall, taking a deep breath. Apparently, he was a masochist.

When he got to the roof, he set his beer on the table and settled himself on a stool. He propped his feet up on the stool to his right and leaned back, enjoying the view above him. Watching the stars, he thought about the past week.

He'd tried to not let Krisi get into his head. Into his heart. But based on his reaction downstairs, he had to admit that campaign had been a failure. She'd joined him and Shelby every day to watch the sunrise. Each morning, they spent a little more time together.

She popped into his office every time she went through the lobby. While they hadn't gone out on a date and neither had made a romantic overture, he felt like they were getting closer. It hadn't occurred to him to ask if she had a boyfriend. It shouldn't have come as a surprise to see she did. And of course, he was someone as sophisticated as Krisi, higher up the social ladder than Brian.

He picked up his beer and took a swig, still staring at the stars. What was he going to do tomorrow if Krisi was waiting to watch the sunrise? It would be petty to end their friendship.

He heard the soft woosh of the elevator doors opening and turned to see who was there. When no one came around the corner, he settled back on his stool.

"Ahem."

The soft clearing of a throat startled him. He looked over to find Krisi next to the table with a bottle of wine and two glasses.

"You left before I could introduce you to my brother."

"Your...your brother. Oh." The vice around his heart loosened a few notches, but now he felt like a heel for avoiding them in the elevator. While the tension in his chest might have eased, there was another kind of tension just having her in his space.

"You don't mind if I join you, do you?" Krisi was standing next to the table, watching him, her lower lip caught between her teeth.

"No...of course." He awkwardly pulled his feet off the stool and stood, his brain slowly catching up to the situation. He picked up the wine and looked at the label. "Good wine," he said, not mentioning it was his favorite.

"Shelby recommended it." She grinned and accepted the glass he offered. "So what're you doing up here?" She looked around the familiar area.

They'd spent every morning here since that first sunrise. He wondered how different this spot looked to her at night. In the dark. He had party lights that he'd kept unlit to match his dark mood.

"I needed fresh air," he answered truthfully. Since meeting her at the farmers' market, Krisi had lodged herself in his head and was working her way to his heart. While Brian did well for himself, he wasn't under any illusion she would be interested in him. At least not romantically.

She set her wineglass on the table, stood, and walked closer to the railing to look out at the view. "Wow, it's gorgeous up here at night too." She shivered a little, reminding him her outfit probably wasn't the warmest.

"You chilly?"

"Just a little." She shrugged it off.

He stood, took off his leather jacket, and draped it around her shoulders.

"Thanks." She smiled at him and pulled the jacket tight around her body. "I didn't think to change before coming up." She moved a little closer to the edge of the roof. "This view is incredible."

He walked over to stand next to her. "It's a whole new world up here, isn't it?"

The view *was* magnificent. To the east was mostly suburban Nashville and the mountains further away. There were pinpricks of light scattered throughout the hills in the distance.

"Want to see the downtown view?" At her nod, he took her hand in his, ignoring the shot of heat running up his arm, and led her to the opposite side of the roof. Her hand was small and cool inside his, but to his mind, it fit perfectly. With his free hand, he used his phone to light their way across the roof.

He led her to the side where the city lights twinkled like a colorful blanket of stars. The skyline stretched before them, the buildings tall and proud. It looked so different at night.

He pointed to a short building not far away. "There's the Country Music Hall of Fame. Every once in a while, you can hear music when they have a concert. And there"—he pointed to a cluster of colorful lights beaming up from behind that building—"is LoBro."

"Mmm." Her soft hum set off another rush of sensations from his ears to his chest. "The lights are mesmerizing from this height. So different from being down in the chaos."

He chuckled. "For sure." LoBro, or Lower Broadway, was not his favorite area to hang out these days, but it was fun to watch from afar. He pointed a little further away. "There's the pedestrian bridge and the stadium just beyond that. But my favorite," he said with a grin, pointing to the AT&T Building off to the left, "is the Batman building."

Her laugh tickled his ears. "When I was in Paris, I met someone who called it La Bat Tower. Now every time I see it, I think *La Bat Tower.*"

She said it with a French accent and flair, making him smile. Their gazes locked and held, as if neither of them wanted to be the first to look away.

From below, the sounds of the city drifted up on a gentle breeze—the hum of traffic, the laughter of people enjoying themselves, occasionally music from one of the many bars lining Broadway. But here, many stories above the city, it was peaceful. Brian felt as though they were the only two people in the world, cocooned in their own private oasis.

As they stood, looking at the city, his city, everything seemed different. They'd been building a friendly relationship during their short time together, but tonight there was new tension. The air between them felt charged, making him wonder *what* was changing. He wondered if he was the only one who felt it.

Krisi turned and stared into his eyes. "Brian, I...I feel like there's something here. Do you feel it too?"

"Friendship?" Brian's voice came out squeaky, and he broke the link between their eyes, afraid she would see everything he was feeling, keenly aware of how far out of his league she was. It didn't pay to even dream about anything more with her.

But as he looked at her in the soft glow of the city lights, he wondered. Hoped.

"Friendship..." Her lips turned down with a small frown. "Is that all you want?"

Of course he wanted more. Should he even mention it? Did she want more? He looked into her eyes again. "Well...I—"

Before he could say anything more, she took a step forward. Closer.

The air between them seemed to thicken as his breath caught in his throat. More than anything, he wanted to reach out, to pull her close. To feel her in his arms.

"I just asked," she said softly, leaning forward ever so slightly. "Because I would like more."

Her soft, warm hands came up to frame his chilly face. Their breath mingled as her eyes searched his. She closed the slight gap between them, pressing her bright pink lips firmly against his.

Any thoughts racing through his brain came to a screeching stop. His eyes automatically closed, and colors, like a firecracker, popped behind his lids.

This kiss was cautious and only lasted a few seconds, but it changed everything in Brian.

She pulled away from him, and the world, which had been temporarily blocked out, rushed back in. The cool night air enveloped them once again, along with the sounds of the city.

Her blue eyes twinkled in the dark. "I need to go, but I hope you'll think about it." She turned and walked to the elevator, her long blond hair fluttering in the breeze.

He stood for several minutes, rooted to the spot. Afraid that if he moved, he'd realize what he'd just experienced wasn't real.

He very much wanted it to be real.

Finally, after the elevator doors closed, he turned and looked at the city lights sprawling in front of him.

Why on earth would an *heiress* want to be in a relationship with him, a nobody? And why, when she could obviously have any man she wanted, would she want *him*?

He would most certainly be thinking about what she said. He had no doubt it would keep him up all night.

Chapter 9

KRISI

Three wishes:

- *I wish I was going to the gala with Brian.*

- *Patience while Brian makes his decision.*

- *Evade Senator Black at the gala.*

T HE NEXT EVENING, KRISI walked into the ballroom where the gala was being held, feeling good about life in general. She'd told Brian that she liked him and wanted more than friendship. It was a bold move, and she hoped she hadn't scared him. Like a schoolgirl, she'd slept with his leather jacket next to her pillow, his woodsy scent keeping her company all night as she tossed and turned.

The kiss had been meant to be light and fun, something for Brian to think about. Instead, it had kept her up all night. The bolt of electricity that raced through her body as soon as her lips touched his had scared her.

She didn't get up early that morning to meet him and Shelby to watch the sunrise, partly because she had a busy day, but also because she wasn't ready to hear Brian say he wasn't interested in more than friendship. She wondered if he'd felt anything in the kiss. If it affected him even half as much as it had her.

The ballroom, on the top floor of the hotel, was magnificent. Upon entering, she was greeted by the breathtaking sight of crystal chandeliers hung from a high, intricately designed ceiling. Their warm, inviting glow was reflected in the polished marble floor. Elegant silk panels on the walls added another layer of luxury to the room. The cream, gold, and deep blue helped keep the large space from feeling sterile and cold. Along one wall was a bank of floor-to-ceiling windows offering a sweeping view of the city skyline and the mountains in the distance.

At the heart of the ballroom, a spacious dance floor awaited the fun that would come in the evening. The stage at the end of the dance floor would host a popular country singer, allowing guests to show off their line-dance and two-step moves. Round tables draped in fine linens and topped with elegant floral arrangements surrounded the dance floor, and candles her mother had special-ordered would allow guests to enjoy the music and mingle in comfort.

Along one of the walls, a full-service bar stood surrounded by a host of volunteers who had spent months organizing the event. She spotted her mother in the center of the crowd and made her way across the room.

Her mother was meticulously dressed. Her long black gown was simple, set off with rhinestones around the low-cut neckline and draped across the open back. The dress had long, sheer sleeves to add an interesting element to her look.

"Mother, you look stunning, as always." Krisi leaned in to kiss her mother's cheek.

"Kristine, darling, look at you." She held Krisi at arm's length and looked her up and down. Krisi was used to her mother's scrutiny and put on a pleasant smile.

"Interesting color choice." Her mother frowned at Krisi's aqua pantsuit. The palazzo style pants draped softly to the floor, almost looking like a skirt. Her jacket was fitted, came to her hips, and with only a teal bra underneath, it was daring but not overly revealing. A long diamond necklace fell to the base of her sternum.

"Thank you," Krisi replied, knowing it wasn't meant as a compliment.

"I never understand why you don't just wear black."

Krisi held back an eyeroll and instead gave her mother a small smile. "I suppose I feel these events need a little sunshine sprinkled amongst all the black. Anyway, I know you're busy, so what can I do to help?"

"I would love a glass of water. Would you be a dear and get it for me?" Her mother turned and headed away without waiting for an answer.

As encounters with her mother went, Krisi considered this one successful. Her real goal for the evening was to avoid her father and Senator Black as much as possible. She turned and made her way to the bar, stopping along the way to say hello to several of her mother's friends who were helping with the final setup as well.

"Krisi, dear. So good to see you." One of the matriarchs of Nashville society leaned in for air kisses. "I heard you were back in town."

"Hello, Mrs. Kinzinger, good to see you." Krisi smiled at the older woman.

She leaned in and lowered her voice. "I also heard you were seen with that handsome senator?"

"Oh!" It always surprised Krisi how quickly information got around the city. "I did have lunch with Senator Black the other day." The last thing she wanted was rumors flying about her and the senator.

"You might want to snag him quickly," Mrs. Kinzinger cackled. "He's one of the most eligible bachelors in town."

Krisi plastered on a gracious smile. "I'm sure he'll be a wonderful catch for someone, but not me. It was great to see you again, Mrs. Kinzinger."

Krisi extricated herself from the conversation and finally made it to the bar. With a glass of water for her mother, she turned and found herself face-to-face with the exact person she was hoping to avoid.

"Krisi." Senator Black's voice slithered across her body, making her shiver. This time, his gaze did wander down her body.

"Senator." She made sure her smile was in place, pulling his eyes back to hers. "Lovely to see you." Seeing he was leaning in for a kiss, she turned back to the bartender to say thank you, then turned back around to see his frown. "I need to get this to my mother."

She quickly made her way to the other side of the room, where she'd last seen her mother. After searching for several minutes, she spotted her talking with a group of women.

"There you are, Kristine." Her mother took the glass from her and took a healthy drink. "Ugh, water. I wish you'd brought me a chilled glass of white wine."

Krisi opened her mouth to point out the obvious, that her mother hadn't asked for wine, but closed it again. It would do no good to point anything out. Instead, she smiled. "It looks like the waiters are making their way around. I'm sure you can get a glass of wine from one of them."

Krisi knew her role at these events. As a family, they supported their mother's efforts to make money for her chosen charity.

She made her way to the silent auction area to check out the offerings. She bid on a couple items and took note of a few others to mention to certain guests. Then it was time to make the rounds and make sure the movers and shakers were having a good time.

"Mrs. Marshall," Krisi said, leaning forward to exchange air kisses with an older woman who looked stunning in a long pale peach dress. "It's good to see you."

Mrs. Gigi Chiapini-Marshall was one of the few society women Krisi genuinely enjoyed. They'd worked on a couple of projects together over the years, and it was always a pleasure to speak with her.

"Krisi, I didn't realize you were back in Nashville. I'm always happy to see someone else not in black." She chuckled. "And I'm pretty sure I've asked you at least a dozen times to call me Gigi."

"I'll try, but no promises." Krisi grinned at the woman who was old enough to be her grandmother. "As for my outfit, Mother wasn't nearly as thrilled with the color choice." She shrugged.

"Bless her heart. She's a stickler for black, isn't she" Mrs. Marshall grinned back at her. "Are you sticking around Nashville for a while?"

For the first time in a long time, Krisi *wanted* to stay in her hometown. Settling down didn't feel as stifling as it had before. She was fairly certain Brian had something to do with the feeling, but she was also interested in spending more time with Alex and Lily.

"I'm hoping to stick around. Actually, I recently moved into an apartment at The Athenian. It's such a beautiful building."

Mrs. Marshall raised an eyebrow. "And how are your parents taking to you living in the city?"

Nashville was a small town sometimes.

Krisi leaned in and lowered her voice. "They were fine with me galivanting around Europe on my own at twenty-two, but living across town at thirty-two seems to be an issue." She rolled her eyes. She didn't normally complain about family to anyone, especially at one of these events, but she trusted Mrs. Marshall to keep it to herself.

"Tom, darling." Mrs. Marshall looped her arm through her husband's and pulled him into the conversation. "Look who's back in town."

"Krisi." Mr. Marshall looked genuinely happy to see her as he leaned down to kiss her cheek. "It's good to see you."

She enjoyed the spicy citrus scent—she was pretty sure it was Old Spice—she always associated with him.

"Good to see you too, Mr. Marshall. Did you happen to notice the whiskey collection on auction?"

He cocked his head and looked at the displays. "I haven't had a chance to look at the items yet. Good whiskey?"

"I think I saw something about a James Bond collection." Krisi grinned as his eyes went wide.

"Excuse me, ladies. Krisi it was good to see you. Gigi, I'll be back in a bit. I have some whiskey to check out."

As he headed toward the auction, Mrs. Marshall laughed. "That'll keep him busy for a while. So tell me, how are you keeping busy now you're back in town? Any interesting men in your life?"

Krisi's mind immediately went to Brian. She was so curious about how he'd responded to her kiss. "No, no one at the moment." She wasn't prepared to share her feelings with anyone yet, especially at an event like this.

Mrs. Marshall leaned forward a bit. "You seem to have an admirer in the room," she said in a low voice. At Krisi's confused look, she continued, "There's a certain senator who hasn't taken his eyes off you since we started talking."

Krisi glanced over her shoulder to see Senator Black in conversation with her father. She wondered, not for the first time, what was going on between the two of them.

"Hmm," she said.

After chatting for a couple more minutes, she excused herself and continued to make her way through the crowd. She was talking to another couple when the senator approached her.

"Excuse me for interrupting, Ms. St. Claire. I think you owe me a dance."

She knew her father would be watching them, so refusing wasn't an option. "Of course, Senator." She smiled and excused herself from the people she'd been talking to, then turned to him. "Shall we?"

He nodded and put his hand on the small of her back, and she was glad her shoulders and back were completely covered. She didn't want his hands on her skin at any point. Just the thought made her skin crawl.

They made their way to the dance floor, where he put an arm around her waist and pulled her close. She settled her hand in his, and they began waltzing.

"If I didn't know better, I'd think you're avoiding me tonight."

His cheek was settled at the side of her head, and his words tickled her ear. It took all her composure to not shiver. Instead, she pulled back, putting space between them.

"Now why would you think that, Senator?"

"You've barely said two words to me tonight." He pouted.

"While it would be lovely to just hang out and talk to one person all night, I'm afraid it's not possible. I'm sure you're aware this is my mother's event. I'm expected to work the room. You know how these things are."

They twirled in silence for a minute or two before she spoke again. "So, Senator, how was your week?"

"Much better now that I have you in my arms." He gracefully twirled her out then brought her back to his arms. "And how was *your* week?"

Thinking of the previous evening, she smiled. "It ended on a high note." She realized by his slight smile, he thought she was talking about him, about now, making her regret her comment. Her mind wandered to the previous evening. She wondered how it would feel to be in Brian's arms, twirling around the dance floor. She smiled at the thought.

"Listen." He interrupted her thoughts and pulled her closer. "I have access to a cabin in the mountains next weekend. I intend to spend every moment possible with you. Shall I pick you up Friday afternoon?" He looked at her, confident in his charm and her answer.

"Senator, that's a very sweet, if presumptuous, offer, but I'm afraid I won't be sharing a cabin in the mountains with you."

Krisi watched as he carefully adjusted his expression. For the briefest of moments, she could have sworn she saw a flash of anger.

"Oh." He paused. "I should have guessed you already have plans."

"I have no idea whether I have plans, Senator. What I do know is, I met you only four days ago. Why would you think I want to go away for a weekend with you?"

He stopped dancing and looked at her. She could feel energy coming off him. Frustration? Anger? She wasn't sure, but it was strong.

Realizing people were beginning to stare, he grabbed her hand, a little too tightly, and led her off to a corner of the room.

"I apologize," he said quietly. "I felt an immediate connection to you and thought it was mutual. I'm happy to take this at your pace, Kristine."

She pulled her hand from his grip and looked at him, frustrated with the direction he was trying to take them. "Senator, I'm sorry if

I gave you the impression I was interested in a relationship. I'm afraid there's someone else in my life."

"Excuse me, Senator." Alex stepped next to her. "I'm going to need to steal my sister away from you."

The senator immediately held his hand out to shake Alex's. "Good to see you, Alexander."

They shook hands, but Alex didn't say anything more. Instead, he nodded and put his arm around Krisi's shoulder to lead her away.

Alex leaned closer. "Sorry I couldn't get to you sooner, but I was waylaid."

She nodded but didn't say anything.

He led her out of the ballroom to a small seating area away from the crowds. She fell onto the couch next to him and rubbed her wrist.

"The good senator seemed very intent in his conversation with you," Alex said. "What was that all about?"

"For some reason, Senator Black seems to think I want to go away for the weekend with him." She shook her head. "We've had lunch

once, and he's already planning a weekend together?"

Alex scrunched his nose. "You going?"

"*Ew*. Of course not. Thank you for rescuing me." She leaned forward to give him a
kiss on the cheek. "Have you seen Lily?" Krisi
hadn't seen her younger sister at all, which was
weird.

"I saw her briefly. Our good senator tried to
corner her, but she "accidentally" spilled some
wine on her dress and had to leave."

Krisi laughed. "I'll have to remember that
for my next encounter with the man. Lessons
from Lily." She shook her head, grinning. Her
admiration for her sister ramped up a notch.

"I think I'll go back in, do one more round
of chatting up the crowd, then head out myself. I'm not keen to get cornered again."

As they headed into the ballroom, Krisi
wondered if Brian would be willing to join her
at events like this. She grinned thinking about
him in a tuxedo. He would look stunning.

She blew out a breath. This was part of her
life, part of her family's tradition. Would he be
comfortable at such an extravagant event?

Chapter 10

BRIAN

BRIAN TRIED TO CONVINCE himself he wasn't waiting up for Krisi, but he was. He'd been disappointed when she hadn't joined him that morning. For the first time in a while, he watched the sunrise alone. Shelby had opted to sleep in since her work schedule kept her up late. He used to revel in watching the sunrise by himself, but this morning, it felt lonely. He missed spending that early morning time with Krisi.

She'd asked him to think about if he wanted more than friendship. He'd done nothing but think about it. Since the moment he'd met her. Now that he knew she wanted more...

well, she'd certainly done a good job of keeping him up all night. Whether it had been her goal or not.

He'd seen Krisi when she left for her mother's event. She'd looked stunning in a pale blue-green outfit. He wondered if she enjoyed high society events. He wondered if he would. He shook his head, no reason to get ahead of himself.

Looking at his spotless desk, he sighed, realizing there was nothing left to work on. Which meant he had no more excuses to stay here until Krisi returned. He powered down his computer just as he heard the lobby doors open. He made a quick about-face and decided to take the elevator to his apartment instead of the stairs. After tucking his laptop into his bag, he picked up his keys and stepped out of his office just in time to see Krisi with a man who looked to be in his early fifties, wearing what was surely a custom-made tuxedo.

This is the type of man Krisi belongs with. He sighed to himself.

"Ms. St. Claire." He nodded to her, then turned to lock the office door. For a split second, he questioned whether or not he should take the elevator.

Confusion blurred his mind, making him wonder if the kiss and her declaration the evening before had even happened.

"Have a good evening, Senator," Krisi said loudly, making Brian decide the lobby elevator was exactly where he wanted to be. He tucked his insecurities aside and smiled to himself. A little sapling of hope sprouted.

"A gentleman walks a lady to her door," the man said smoothly as Brian joined them in front of the elevator.

"That won't be necessary. Thank you for the ride home." She made to turn away from him, but he caught her wrist and spun her around to face him.

"There's no reason to play coy, Kristine."

His face was close to Krisi's, his voice low. He ran a finger down her cheek.

Brian felt his fists clench and his shoulders tense.

"We both know how this evening is going to end."

Krisi pulled her head back and looked at her wrist. "You're going to want to remove your hand from me, Senator."

He looked at her wrist and slowly unwound his fingers, but he maintained his position in front of her. Brian watched as she rubbed her red wrist. It took all his willpower to not push this man—this senator—away from Krisi.

Either he hadn't noticed Brian or didn't see him as a threat to his evening plans. Brian's blood began to simmer as he watched. The fact that the man thought it was okay to leave a mark on Krisi—or any woman—was infuriating. He was about to speak when Krisi continued.

"Yes, Senator, I know how this evening is going to end." She looked at him with steely eyes. "I'm going to my apartment. Alone. My father may have maneuvered me into letting you give me a ride home, but it doesn't extend any further than here."

The elevator dinged. With her back to the doors, Krisi almost fell into the elevator when the doors opened.

Brian stepped around the man and reached out his hand, but Krisi had already caught herself. Brian stepped into the elevator behind her, then turned to face the open door, positioning himself between Krisi and the senator.

The senator took a step to enter the elevator and, for the first time, seemed to notice Brian. He put his hand on Brian's arm to move him aside but found him to be immovable. Jerking to an abrupt stop so he wouldn't slam into the hulking body, the man sneered at Brian's stoic face.

"Move aside. You're in my way."

"Not that she needs my help, but the lady has made it clear she doesn't want you to go up to her apartment." Brian folded his arms across his thick chest.

"Do you know who I am?" His eyes narrowed as he stared at Brian. "This is none of your business, and you *don't* want to get in my way." The senator's face hardened as he waited for Brian to move.

"It sounds like you're a senator," Brian said nonchalantly.

"That's right. Senator Michael Black."

Brian raised an eyebrow. Oh yes, he'd heard of this man. Brian hadn't voted for him. The man wielded power in the state senate like a sword.

"Oh good. You've heard of me." He seemed to take Brian's awareness as fear. "If you don't move aside, I'll have your job. I happen to know the owner of this building and will have you out of here by morning."

Brian couldn't help the scoff that escaped. He reached over and pushed the button to close the doors. "Have a good evening, Senator."

The doors closed in the senator's face, and Brian looked at Krisi for the first time. Her back was flat against the far wall of the elevator, and she had a concerned expression on her pale face.

"I'm sorry if I overstepped," he said softly. "But there was no way I was letting him in the elevator with you."

She shook her head. "No, I appreciate it, but you've just made an enemy, Brian. He could easily get you fired from here."

Brian grinned at her. "Trust me, he doesn't know the owner. I'll be fine." The doors opened on the sixth floor, and he held it for her. "I missed watching the sunrise with you this morning. I hope to see you tomorrow."

She stopped in front of him and looked into his eyes. "I appreciate your help tonight. I'm not going to set an alarm in the morning, but if I wake up, I'll see you." She briefly placed a hand on his cheek.

Brian leaned into her soft warm palm. He was hoping she'd close the gap between them so he could *show* her his answer to her question. He *really* wanted to be more than friends with her.

But all too soon, her hand was back at her side. She stepped out of the elevator and walked to her apartment without looking back.

Brian let the doors close, his hand involuntarily reaching for his cheek, still warm from her touch. He pushed the button to go back to the lobby, wanting to make sure Black had left. He knew the senator couldn't access the elevator without a key card, so Krisi was safe

for the evening and wouldn't be bothered by
the man.

The doors opened to an empty lobby. Brian stepped out and waited for the doors to
close before moving around the lobby. He
walked down the hall to the only open business, Uncorked, and did a sweep of the customers, then headed back to the elevator.
When the doors opened again, he stepped inside and pushed the button for the second
floor.

He was glad he'd waited up for Krisi.
He didn't even want to imagine what might
have happened if the senator had made it to
her apartment. He shook his head to get the
thoughts out of his head.

One thing he knew, the evening's events
helped him solidify his feelings for Krisi. And
if she joined him in the morning, he was ready
to share that news with her.

Chapter 11

KRISI

KRISI WASN'T PLEASED WHEN her phone buzzed her awake at five o'clock. She planned to sleep in, then enjoy a cup of coffee downstairs, so she let it go to voicemail. When the buzzing started again seconds later, she opened her eyes just enough to see *Daddy* as the caller's ID.

Ugh.

"Hello," she answered groggily.

"What in the world were you thinking last night?" he asked without preamble.

"Excuse me?" Krisi let out a silent sigh, knowing this wouldn't be a fun conversation.

"I got a call from Senator Black at three o'clock this morning telling me how rude you were to him."

"What?" Krisi sat up in bed. Why in the world was the senator running to her father? And at three o'clock in the morning?

"I'm on my way over to discuss this."

"No," she said quickly. "Sorry, Daddy, but I have an early coffee appointment. I can meet you for lunch." She was not going to let her father control her schedule. She held her breath as she awaited his response.

"One o'clock at the club," he said before hanging up.

She shook her head at the weird wake-up call but raised a fist at her small victory. Standing up for herself against her father was challenging, but she'd just taken an important first step.

And since she was awake, she was ready for another important step.

Sunrise with Brian.

She'd given him a day to think about the fact that she wanted more from their relationship. Now she wanted to see what those thoughts of his were. She hoped he wanted more. She thought about the events of the previous evening, how calm and collected Brian had been while facing Senator Black. When he'd stepped into the elevator with her and blocked the doors, flutters had held her in place against the wall. She'd never felt so protected as she had in that moment, and it had been powerful for her. Not only had her feelings for Brian ramped up, but so had her respect for him at standing up to a powerful man. She hoped the senator didn't retaliate.

Before climbing out of bed, she wrapped her fingers around the charm and thought about her three wishes.

- *More than friendship*

- *Good lunch with Daddy*

- *Truth comes out about Senator Black*

After hopping out of bed, Krisi pulled her hair into a messy bun, dressed in a warm lounge outfit, grabbed a coat, and headed out the door for the elevator. She loved that she didn't have to dress up to meet Brian for sunrise. It was come as you are, and he didn't judge her for not being *camera ready*, as her mother called it.

The doors opened on the second floor to reveal Brian standing there with two coffees. She couldn't keep the grin off her face. He hadn't commented on her bold kiss or her declaration, but he'd made her a cup of coffee.

"Good morning." He smiled as he entered the elevator and handed her an insulated mug. "I was hoping you'd join me." He pushed the button for the roof and relaxed against the wall. "You sleep okay? I wasn't sure if you were going to wake up early or not today."

"I got a wake-up call from my father." She grimaced, thinking about Senator Black calling him at three in the morning. "I hate that he woke me up, but I'm happy to take advantage of it by starting my day with you." She held up the mug he'd handed her. "And with a delicious cup of your coffee."

His grin matched her feelings. Something had shifted between them. The fact that he'd been there last night to keep Senator Black from following her to her apartment had been a gift. She wouldn't have been able to physically hold the senator off. That thought scared her.

The doors opened, and the dark rooftop spread out in front of them. They made their way to the table, and she donned her warm jacket before sitting on the stool next to him. She noticed the chairs weren't on opposite sides of the table anymore. They were closer together. Their elbows bumped as they settled in and propped their feet up on the extra stools he'd brought up at some point. She relaxed back with her coffee, ready to watch the show Mother Nature had for them that morning.

Brian looked at her. "So does your father normally wake you up this early?"

She shook her head. "Thankfully, no. Senator Black called him at three this morning. I'm going to hear all about it at lunch." Her stomach dipped as she thought about the impending conversation. Confrontation wasn't her strong suit, but it seemed life was throwing her lots of opportunities to practice.

"Why would Senator Black call your father? At three in the morning? Are they close?" Brian didn't seem concerned, just curious.

Krisi was concerned. She didn't want the senator to ruin Brian's life or livelihood. And the senator had threatened to do exactly that.

"I'm not sure. I haven't kept up with local politics or my father's business interests for a long time. My brother told me the senator recently passed a bill that is quite favorable to my family's business. It wouldn't surprise me if there was some quid pro quo."

Brian paused his mug halfway to his mouth. "What does that have to do with you?"

"I have no idea. Hopefully, I'll get some answers later today. Though my father isn't typically forthcoming with information. Especially to me."

She watched as Brian's forehead scrunched up, but he didn't say anything. They sat in comfortable silence, watching colors shift on the eastern horizon. When the sun was fully up, Brian turned to her again.

"I was wondering..." His fingers drummed on his coffee mug. "If you'd like to go to dinner with me Friday?"

Her heart melted a little to realize he was more nervous about asking her to dinner than he'd been facing off with Senator Black. The fact that he wanted to move forward with their relationship thrilled her.

"I'd love to have dinner with you, Brian." Her stomach fluttered, and her pulse kicked up a beat in anticipation.

"Good." His slow smile did funny things to her stomach. "I'd really like our relationship to be more than friendship too."

Her pulse skipped at hearing those words. Sure, he was different from the other men she'd dated, but maybe that was the point. None of her other relationships had worked; maybe this one would.

Krisi walked into NPS, Nashville Premiere Society, the private club her father had been a member of her whole life. It was elegantly decorated and furnished...and obviously catered to men. The colors were dark, the furniture mostly leather and wood. She walked through the lobby, up the stairs to the concierge desk on the second floor landing, and was admitted entry to the elevator to take her to the top floor where a private restaurant was located.

The only way to become a member of the club was to be invited—which only happened when someone died—or to be born into it. When her father passed away, Alex would inherit the membership. Some of the perks of belonging to the club, besides the prestigious clientele you could rub elbows with, included a whiskey bar, a cigar lounge, a couple of high-end restaurants, and several meeting rooms of various sizes.

Krisi walked into the restaurant and found her father in conversation with another man. She nodded to the hostess and made her way across the room to him. He nodded to acknowledge her presence but continued with his conversation for another couple of minutes. When the conversation ended, the other man left without an introduction.

"Let's find a table and get our orders in." Her father ushered her back across the room to the hostess stand, and they were led to a table. Once they were seated and their drinks ordered, a whiskey for her father, a sparkling water for her, he finally looked at her. "So want to tell me what happened last night?"

"Hi, Krisi," she said in a singsong tone. "Good to see you. Thank you for joining me today."

Her father wasn't amused. "Don't get smart with me." His voice was clipped and hard.

"Since when were manners and normal niceties *getting smart*?" she asked. "Your daughter doesn't even warrant a *hello*?"

She was hurt, but at the same time, she barely recognized her father. He'd become a cold, hard man. He seemed to have more of a connection with Alex, maybe because he was in the family business. Lily was the baby of the family, and he tended to dote on her, but Krisi'd had the audacity to be born first and not male. Frankly, she was getting tired of it.

"Hello, Krisi." He took a long, exasperated breath. "Now what happened with Senator Black? He was very upset last night."

Krisi's eyebrows both went up. "*He* was upset? What in the world was he upset about? *I'm* the one who should be upset."

His salt-and-pepper eyebrows drew together in a scowl. "According to him, you had him thrown out of The Athenian."

Krisi took a deep breath to calm herself. She knew if she responded defensively, he wouldn't listen to her. Fortunately, the waiter arrived with their drinks, and the distraction of ordering gave her time to compose herself. Any outburst would not be tolerated, but the fact that the senator was telling complete lies was frustrating. She closed her eyes and took another centering breath.

"At your insistence, Senator Black gave me a ride home. I thanked him, but he wouldn't leave. He wanted to walk me to my apartment door. I wasn't comfortable with that and told him no. That isn't kicking him out of the building. It's just not letting him into my home."

Her father took a deep drink of whiskey. After setting the tumbler down, he looked at her again. "Why weren't you comfortable with him walking you to your door?"

She wasn't sure whether he was genuinely curious or defending the senator, but she chose to assume the first. "He made me uncomfortable." She held up her bruised wrist for him to see. "When I said no, this is what I got from him."

Her father's eyebrows knit together, and his mouth turned down in a frown. She could tell he was upset. Uncomfortable even.

He leaned forward, his chin resting on his knuckles, but he didn't say anything. Instead, he looked at the ceiling, thinking.

After the waiter served their meals, her father looked back at her. "So how did you get him to leave?"

"The manager of the building happened to be going up in the elevator at the same time." She didn't mention anything about their relationship. This wasn't the time. "He told Senator Black I said no and wouldn't let him on the elevator."

Her father nodded and took a bite of salmon. "He asked me if I knew who was behind SBS Holdings, Inc. It's the company that owns The Athenian."

Krisi gave an unladylike snort into her napkin. "Ha. The senator said he knew the owner and intended to have Brian fired. Doesn't sound like he actually does."

"No, he doesn't."

She was quiet for a moment, thinking about what she'd learned. "Daddy, why did Senator Black call *you* this morning? What's going on?"

Her father was thoughtful now. "Be careful, Krisi. The senator's a dangerous man. He's not someone you want to make an enemy of."

Her father hadn't actually answered her question, but somewhere deep down, she recognized her father was scared. She just wasn't sure if it was for her or for himself.

"I don't want him as an enemy," she said. "I also don't want him as a friend. Most certainly not as a lover." She watched her father blanch at her words. "Lily was right, he's creepy."

The conversation, while it hadn't directly answered her questions, had reopened communication between her and her father. She felt a hint of a connection with him again, and she hoped it would stick around. Maybe even grow.

Chapter 12

BRIAN

AT FIVE O'CLOCK MONDAY afternoon, Brian's phone buzzed. A smile crossed his lips when he saw a text from Krisi.

KRISI: Feel like grabbing dinner?

He'd been kicking himself for setting their date so far in the future. Waiting a whole week to go out with her was proving to be a challenge. Thankfully, Krisi had just solved the dilemma for him.

BRIAN: absolutely

BRIAN: when & where?

KRISI: I'll meet you in the lobby in 45 minutes

Brian hadn't seen Krisi since their sunrise coffee the morning before. He knew she'd had lunch with her father, and he was curious to hear how it had gone. With his evening suddenly looking brighter, he took a shower and changed into clean jeans and a light green polo shirt that, according to Shelby, matched his eyes. Though he wasn't sure why it mattered. He stepped into loafers and walked into the living room.

Shelby was on the couch, reading a book. She looked up, her eyebrow cocked. "Going somewhere?"

"Krisi just texted, and we're going to dinner."

"You said yes?" Shelby's eyes were wide. She knew he was a planner and last minute changes made him anxious.

He rubbed his hands on his jeans, then caught himself and stuck them in his pockets.

Before he could reply, she continued speaking. "Getting serious with Ms. St. Claire?" She waggled her eyebrows.

Brian grinned but shook his head. "No, we're taking it slow. She's so far out of my league, Shelb. I'm not even sure why we're going out."

"Well, I'm guessing because you like her," Shelby said. "And for the record, she is *not* out of your league, Brian Edward Streatt. You may not be heir to a billion-dollar company, but you've created something to be proud of here."

He sat next to his sister and pulled her in for a side hug. "When did you get to be so smart?" He dropped a kiss on her hair. "I appreciate that. Have fun at work tonight. I'll stop by to see you."

He headed out the door to the elevator. When the doors opened at the lobby level, his breath caught at the sight of Krisi in one of the lounge chairs by the front windows. Fading sunlight cast a halo around her body, making her skin glow. She turned her head when the elevator chimed, and her smile took hold of his heart. It seemed to beat a little faster every time he was around her...but at the same time, he felt completely content.

Tonight she wore a pair of jeans, a silky black top, and knee-high black boots. A black leather jacket was slung over the seat next to her. She stood as he came closer, then surprised him by reaching up and touching her lips to his.

A shiver ran from his mouth to just under his ribcage, somewhere in the vicinity of his heart. He took a deep breath and let it out slowly. Her perfume permeated every pore of his body, calming his nerves and clearing his head.

"So." Brian gazed into her sparkling blue eyes and wondered if she knew just how deeply she affected him. "Where to tonight?"

"I'd love Italian." She kept a hand on his arm, maintaining contact with him.

"Sounds good. Got anywhere specific in mind?"

"No." She shook her head, her blond hair swaying behind her. "It's been so long since I've had Italian in Nashville, I'm not even sure what's around."

"I know just the place." And he did. A small family-run restaurant not too far away. He wrapped an arm around her waist and steered her toward the garage. "Want me to drive?"

She stopped and turned her body into his, a twinkle returning to her eyes. "Any chance we can take your motorcycle?"

Brian felt an eyebrow tick up, but he grinned at her adventurous attitude. "Sure. Let me grab keys and helmets."

He went to his office, where he exchanged his truck keys for the bike's, collected his and Shelby's helmets from the bookshelf, and lifted his leather jacket from the back of his chair. With everything tucked under an arm, he re-locked his office door and made his way back to Krisi.

"This is Shelby's. It should fit you better than mine."

She grinned at the pink helmet, then looped her arm through his as they made their way to the garage. Brian put his jacket on and swung a leg over the motorcycle. He waited while Krisi donned her jacket and helmet, then secured the strap beneath her chin. With a hand on his shoulder, she climbed on behind him. This time, she didn't hesitate to wrap her arms around him. He enjoyed the feel of her, snug against his back, as he started the engine and walked the bike out of the parking space. As soon as they pulled out of the garage, she rested her head on his back and tightened her grip around his waist.

It was only a fifteen-minute ride to Amati's in Germantown, but Brian dragged it out as long as possible by taking the scenic route. All too soon, he pulled up in front of the mom-and-pop restaurant and lowered his feet to the ground to stabilize the bike while Krisi stepped off. He set the kickstand and looped the helmets over the handlebars.

It was a short walk along the cobblestone sidewalk, and he laced his fingers through hers, enjoying a sense of belonging. The entrance was a heavy wooden door painted red with a small plaque announcing Amati's at eye level. He pulled open the door, then stepped through behind her to be met by an overwhelming wave of scents that made his stomach grumble. Garlic, onion, yeasty bread, and sweet tomato sauce. A powerful combination of aromas.

"Oh my stars." Krisi looked at him, her hand on her stomach. "It smells so good in here."

"Always does."

Mrs. Amati bustled over and welcomed them. Krisi lingered at the small market set up in the lobby, looking at some pottery.

"Go ahead," she said to Brian. "I'll be out in a minute."

Brian grinned as he spotted a couple he knew in the small dining area. The woman stood as soon as he got close.

"Brian, it's so good to see you." She leaned in and hugged him. Her red, wavy hair smushed against his cheek.

"Breena, it's great to see you too." He turned and held out a hand to her husband, Gabriel's new wedding band gleaming in the candlelight. "Gabriel, good to see you as well. I have to say, I miss seeing you both at The Athenian."

Brian had attended their Valentine's Day wedding. As happy as he was for them, he was always sad when residents of his community moved away.

Breena grinned. "I miss seeing you too. Are you dining alone? Pull up a chair and join us."

"Oh, thanks, but no. I've got a date." He could feel his cheeks warm. He wasn't embarrassed to be seen with Krisi—far from it—but this was the first time he'd used the word *date* in relation to her. *Were* they dating? He had no idea. He chatted another minute before returning to the entryway just as Krisi stepped into the dining room.

She took hold of his hand as they made their way through the tables. Brian loved the restaurant's homey atmosphere. The tables were simple—red checkered cloths, candles stuck in wine bottles, two wineglasses waiting to be filled.

Krisi squeezed his hand. "Go ahead. I'd like to say hi to Breena."

He nodded and walked to the table Mrs. Amati had set their menus on. The dining area was small, only about a dozen tables, so they were only a few steps away from Breena and Gabe.

Mrs. Amati came over with two water glasses. "I'll be right back with breadsticks."

As soon as Krisi finished her conversation, Brian stood to meet her.

"What's so funny?" he asked as he pulled her chair out.

She chuckled. "Breena was surprised that I was your date."

He noticed she used the word *date* as well.

"To be fair, Breena hasn't really seen me out with anyone since I've known her." Brian shrugged. "How do you know her?"

"I met her when she and Grace looked at my cabin in the mountains. Breena had driven them up in her little sports car, and when it started to snow, she was nervous to drive back down the mountain. I wound up giving them both a lift home." Krisi chuckled at the memory. "So how's it been for you since she and Grace moved out?"

"It's kind of weird not seeing them all the time, but that's the nature of the business. People come, people go. Our community shifts and changes."

"Grace said she sold her penthouse to Laci Love." Krisi leaned forward, her attention focused on him. "Has she moved in yet? I haven't seen her."

"I think her European tour is finishing soon, so I imagine we'll start seeing her around sooner or later."

"I would enjoy meeting her. I caught her concert in Paris before moving back to Nashville. She puts on one heck of a show."

Mrs. Amati came back with a basket of bread and a bottle of red wine. "Compliments of Gabriel and Breena." She opened the bottle and poured some in each glass.

Brian grinned and raised his glass to Gabriel. "Tell them thank you. We'll enjoy it."

He figured Breena was probably curious about him and Krisi being on a date...well, he was curious too.

She lifted her glass and touched it to his. "Thanks for coming out with me tonight. I'm in need of a friend after lunch with my father yesterday."

Brian kept the smile on his face but felt disappointment lodge in his stomach at her use of *friend*. His fingers tightened on his wineglass, and he took a sip, reminding himself the friend zone was probably the safer route anyway. He refocused his attention just in time to hear Krisi mention the senator's early morning call to her father.

"I wonder why he'd call your father, especially at that hour."

The whole scene at The Athenian with Senator Black hadn't sat well with Brian. He didn't know the man and had never interacted with him, but it had left him troubled. Like it wasn't finished between them. Now he could see it wasn't.

Krisi shook her head. "I'm not sure what's going on with my father and the senator or why I'm in the middle of it. I don't like it. And it turns out, he doesn't know the owner of The Athenian."

Brian grinned and shook his head. "I wasn't concerned about that."

"He's a dangerous man, Brian." He could hear concern in her tone and knew she was right, but he was more worried for her than for himself.

Dinner was a delicious, leisurely affair. They talked about everything and nothing. It

surprised Brian how easy it was to be with
Krisi. She didn't *seem* like an heir...not that he
knew what that should look like. She shared
funny stories about starting her perfume company overseas and some of the laughable lan-
guage mix-ups she'd encountered. It hadn't
been easy, especially since she didn't want to
use family money.

The longer they talked, the more Brian forgot how wrong they were for each other. How
different she was from him. Instead, he found
himself relating to her and discovering parallels
in business decisions they'd both made over
the years. Working hard to make their dreams
come true.

He'd limited his wine to a half a glass, but
while walking out of the restaurant with Krisi
holding his hand, his whole body felt ener-
gized. Buzzy almost. The cool air on the ride
back to The Athenian helped clear his head,
and by the time he pulled into the underground garage, he was feeling in control again.

He stood in the elevator with his back to
the wall, Krisi leaning against him, her head on
his chest.

"Thank you for going to dinner with me tonight," she said softly. She reached a hand up and rubbed the charm on her necklace.

"I'll go to dinner with you anytime." He wrapped his arms around her and kissed the side of her head. "What's on your necklace?"

She turned her head to look up at him, her lips almost colliding with his. "It's my genie lamp. My Grandma Annie gave it to me when I was sixteen."

He looked at the charm and could see it was indeed a genie's lamp. "Do you make wishes on your lamp?"

"Actually, yes. Every morning before I get out of bed, I rub my lamp and make three wishes."

He grinned at her morning routine and wondered if one day he might be one of her three wishes.

The next morning, after spending the early hour on the rooftop watching the sunrise with Krisi, Brian was whistling when he stepped

into his office. He shuffled through the mail
on the corner of his desk, tossing most of it
into the recycle bin. At the bottom of the
pile was a copy of the *Nashville Daily*, which
was odd since he didn't subscribe to it.

He flipped through the pages of the first
section, but not finding anything of import,
he moved on to the People & Scene section. There, on the first page of that section, was a picture of him and Krisi from the
evening before. They were holding hands
while walking from the restaurant to his motorcycle.

The Heiress & the Streatt Rat

Rumor has it Kristine St. Claire
has been cut off from her family
funds. Kristine is the granddaugh-
ter of George St. Claire, the de-
ceased founder of St. Claire Industries, and heir to the family for-
tune along with her younger siblings Alexander and Lilliana. But it

seems Kristine just can't stay out of the papers.

I'm sure dallying with Brian Streatt, a doorman at The Athenian, won't get her back in the good graces of her father. We thought she was keeping company with Senator Michael Black, but her standards seemed to have dive-bombed since moving back to Nashville.

Instead of spending time with the esteemed senator, she was seen out and about in Georgetown last night with Streatt. What in the world is she thinking? Maybe she should move back to Europe, at least the quality of her men was higher there—royalty, movie stars, even a racecar driver.

The article went on to detail the men Krisi dated in Europe, but Brian threw the paper to his desk. Frustrated at seeing his fears spelled out in front of him in black and white, he ran his fingers through his hair.

He didn't need the paper to say he wasn't worthy of Krisi. He already knew it. Now what?

"Hey there, handsome." He looked up to see Krisi in the doorway. Her eyes narrowed and a look of concern crossed her face. "What's wrong?"

"Oh...nothing." He quickly folded the paper and tossed it into the recycle bin.

She stepped forward and reached down to pluck the paper out of the bin. *Shoot!* Brian had hoped to spare her. He watched as she unfolded the paper. Her eyes went wide at the picture and headline.

"I didn't see anyone taking pictures. Did you?" She didn't look happy.

He shook his head. He had zero experience with reporters. Or paparazzi, he supposed.

"I was good at spotting them in Europe. Guess I didn't think to keep an eye out here."

"Krisi, I..." Brian wasn't sure what to say. "I'm sorry it was caught on camera. It was never my intention to embarrass you."

"Embarrass?" Krisi looked genuinely confused. She held up the paper. "While I don't enjoy having my relationships splashed across these pages, Brian, all those 'acceptable' men I dated in Europe were lousy humans." She used air quotes to make her point. "They might have been filthy rich, but they treated people horribly, including me." She shook her head. "I see going out with you as a big step *up* in life, but I don't expect someone from the *Daily* to understand that. Hopefully, you do." She stepped closer to him.

"I..." He had no idea how to respond, but his chest swelled at her comment. "Thank you. I certainly understand you probably don't want this type of scrutiny of your life."

She took another step closer to him, put her hands on the armrests on either side of his chair, and leaned in. "It's not the scrutiny that bothers me, it's *who* is leading the charge." She leaned closer still and briefly touched her lips to his, then she turned and plopped down into his lap. "So the real question is, *who* is doing this? Only one person comes to mind."

"Senator Black?" His arms automatically wrapped around her waist. Her scent made it hard to concentrate on the conversation.

She nodded and turned to face him. "What I don't understand is *why*. Why does the senator care who I go out with?"

"I have to assume he's upset it's not him. He made it clear the other night that he was interested in you."

She looked at the newspaper, still in her grip, again. "*Streatt Rat*? What's that supposed to mean? I mean, I know your last name is Streatt, but..."

"Are they trying to be clever? Like an Aladdin reference?"

She laughed. "Oh! So you're the *street rat* Aladdin. Does that make me Princess Jasmine?"

"I don't know...you don't really have the tiger for it," he joked.

"You haven't met my assistant, Nikki, yet." She chuckled and leaned against his chest. "If you're Aladdin and I'm Jasmine, who does that make the senator?"

Brian raised an eyebrow. "Nobody flattering to him, that's for sure."

Chapter 13

KRISI

Three wishes:

- *Music City Mocha.*

- *A kiss from Brian.*

- *Friendship with Grace.*

THE NEXT MORNING, KRISI raced into
Melody Brews ten minutes late for an

appointment with Grace. She saw a cup of Music City Mocha already on the table, awaiting her arrival.

"I'm sorry I'm late." Krisi heaved herself into the chair and looked at the coffee. "Is this for me?"

"Melody said it's your favorite."

"Thank you." Krisi picked up the mug and took a lifesaving sip. "Ahh, so much better. Okay. I'm ready to jump in."

"Guess who agreed to be in the auction?" Grace asked with a twinkle in her eyes.

Krisi's eyes narrowed then went wide. "Alex? No!"

Grace grinned. "The one and only Alexander St. Claire."

"Oh my stars! I can't believe he said yes. I don't know what you said to him, but well done, Grace."

At that moment, Brian came into the café and captured Krisi's attention. She followed him with her eyes from the doorway to the counter, enjoying the purposeful way he moved his body.

"Earth to Krisi." Grace laughed.

Krisi looked back to Grace and felt her cheeks getting warm. "Sorry." She was acting like a middle school girl with her first crush. It was mortifying.

"That's okay. Brian's a good distraction," Grace said.

Krisi had talked to Nikki about everything going on with Brian, but Nikki wasn't in a relationship. Instead, Nikki was pining for Krisi's oblivious brother. She glanced at the counter, then returned her attention to Grace. It was nice to have someone to talk to about him.

"He's such a good man." Krisi sighed.

"Brian? He is! So what's your hesitation?"

"I get the feeling he's sometimes uncomfortable with my wealth."

"Hmm." Grace looked to the counter then back again. "I'm a little surprised by that."

Brian stopped by their table after getting his coffee.. "Mornin', ladies." He stopped next to Krisi's chair and looked at her. "I just realized why you looked familiar, Krisi. We met very briefly at Christmas. You ran into Grace in the lobby." He looked pleased with himself for sorting it out.

"Oh my gracious!" Krisi exclaimed. "You're right. I can't believe I forgot about that."

"Brian, we were just talking about you," Grace said.

Krisi's gaze drilled a hole into Grace. Surely she wasn't going to share their conversation with him.

Brian's brow quirked up. "All good things, I hope."

"I'm glad you'll be in the bachelor auction," Grace said smoothly.

His hand lingered on Krisi's shoulder, spreading warmth through her body. *This* is what she was interested in, this *feeling* he gave her. Steady. Calm. Love? The thought startled her. *Am I falling in love?*

Brian grinned. "You two have a good morning."

Krisi corralled her thoughts and continued their conversation after he walked away. "Most of the men I've dated have come into the relationship with their own money." She shrugged, not sure what to say. She couldn't change who she was or the family she was born into. "Money doesn't matter to me, but I guess I always pictured myself with someone who was an entrepreneur, like me."

A frown crossed Grace's face. "Brian does pretty well with The Athenian, right? I mean, he's not a billionaire or anything, but…"

"But it doesn't even matter to me." Even as she said it, Krisi wondered if it were true. *Did* it matter that he wasn't rich? She remembered when she saw him the first day in the café, how disappointed she'd been to learn he was the manager. But she'd changed since then. Right? "I like him regardless of what he does or doesn't make financially."

She told Grace about the newspaper article and how she was trying to figure out who had written it and why. The Nashville press didn't usually pay much attention to her.

"Maybe you should pay the reporter a visit," Grace suggested.

An hour later, after they'd finished their meeting and Grace had left, the idea of paying the reporter a visit was still rolling around in

Krisi's brain. If she really wanted to get to the bottom of this, she needed to figure out who wrote the article.

Back in her apartment, she and Nikki were huddled around Nikki's laptop. They pulled up the website for the *Nashville Daily*, then found the article about Krisi and Brian. Once they found the byline, they called and made an appointment under Nikki's name for that afternoon.

"In the meantime," Krisi said, cleaning up the papers in front of her and putting them in a pink leather satchel. "We have a meeting with Brian about the retail space in the lobby. If you can get the shelving and cabinetry ordered this week, it will be one less thing to think about."

Krisi loved the idea that her business would be located in The Athenian. The residents were *exactly* her target market, and the location was perfect for walk-in traffic.

And Brian would be just across the lobby. The thought of seeing him every day filled her with warmth while butterflies camped out in her stomach. All at the same time. It was a little unsettling.

"Okay, I've got the measurements I need." Nikki closed her folder and hooked the tape measure to her jeans. She was as excited as Krisi about opening a new storefront. She looked at Brian. "Are any of these fixtures staying?"

"The previous tenant owns them. I'm not sure if he's closing his gallery completely or just moving it. I can ask if he'd like to sell."

Krisi walked around looking at the few remaining shelves and wall partitions in the space. She shook her head. "Don't ask yet. I'm not sure they'll fit our design scheme. Nikki and I will work on that this afternoon and let you know by the end of the week."

Brian nodded and made a note in the leather journal he carried. "Okay, no problem. The previous tenant is due to vacate within two weeks, so that'll work well, timing wise."

Each of Krisi's boutiques was a little different. She tried to keep the color scheme but enjoyed bringing in the feel of the host city as much as she could. So London was different from Paris, which was different from Madrid. New York was her only storefront in the US.

She hadn't expected to put one in Nashville. She hadn't really expected to want to *stay* in Nashville. Usually, a month or so was long enough. She glanced at Brian. That tall, beautiful man was the reason she was here, planning to stay in Nashville.

"Okay, I'm out of here." Nikki interrupted her thoughts. "I'll plug these numbers in and get started on the design," she said to Krisi. "Brian, good to see you."

Brian moved a little closer to Krisi as they watched Nikki walk out of the space and through the lobby to the elevator.

"I'm going to visit the reporter who wrote the article about us," Krisi said.

"Are you sure that's wise?" The concern in Brian's tone touched her. "Maybe just let it lie. It'll blow over, right? I can't imagine they'll keep writing about us."

Krisi stopped to consider his words. "Maybe you're right. Maybe it was just a slow news day."

He nodded, relief clear on his face. "I'm sure that's all it was." He moved a step closer and smiled. "Can I convince you to go out with me again tonight?"

"How about instead of going out, we eat in?"

"Sounds good."

He was so close, his warm breath tickled her cheek. Her skin tingled in anticipation.

"Why don't you come by around seven? I'll take care of everything," he said.

"I'll be there with bells on." She leaned in and touched her lips to his. "Now I have to go to work. There's a lot to be done if I'm opening another store."

She walked out with a lighter heart, a spring in her step, and flutters in her stomach as she anticipated dinner later. But between now and then, there were a lot of decisions to be made. By the time she was back in her apartment, Nikki already had a basic design for the new store and the names of a few local artists to work with on decorations.

In each of her stores, the layout was basically the same, but they brought in art from

local women artists to serve as both deco-
ration and merchandise. For Krisi, this was
the fun part—checking out local artisans to
highlight in her boutiques. She was a firm
believer in the aphorism credited to John F.
Kennedy, a rising tide lifting all boats. If she
could help raise awareness and business for
some local artists, all the better.

They spent two hours sorting through
the names Nikki compiled and noted the
ones she wanted to reach out to. The soap-
maker and her sister at the farmers' market
came to Krisi's mind. She'd dig out their
business cards and add them to the list.
Next, they moved on to the hardware for
the boutique. They had specific shelving and
cabinetry they used in all her stores, so she
went through the layout Nikki had come up
with.

She was excited about how the new boutique was already coming together. It felt like
a big deal, making it known this was *her* business in *her* hometown. It was time to show
the world—or at least her father—that she was
more than just a trust fund baby. She was a

successful businesswoman with a chain of successful boutiques around the world.

Chapter 14

BRIAN

BRIAN SAT IN HIS office, shuffling the papers on his desk. He was having a hard time focusing on the numbers he was supposed to be crunching. Instead, his mind was very firmly stuck on Krisi. They'd eaten dinner together almost every night this week. Sometimes it was at his apartment, sometimes hers, but she didn't seem interested in going out in public again. He wondered if she was embarrassed to be seen with him.

Another article had come out with a picture of him and Krisi kissing in the former art gallery space. It had to have been after Nikki finished taking measurements and he and

Krisi were alone. The headline this time read *Is Doorman Looking to Go from Rags to Riches with Local Heiress?* He hadn't bothered to read the article.

Krisi had been upset, which he understood. He was upset too. He wasn't a gold digger! He didn't need or want her money. He'd built a life he loved at The Athenian.

He wondered about the article. It was the same writer as the previous article, but how was the newspaper getting the pictures? Maybe he shouldn't have talked her out of visiting the reporter.

When he and Krisi were together, he didn't doubt she liked him, but since that second article came out, she'd been hesitant about going out in public together.

"Hey there."

He looked up to see Grace Montgomery standing in the doorway to his office. He stood and walked around his desk.

"Hey there, yourself. Come on in." He leaned against his desk with his feet crossed in front of him and pointed to a chair. "You're a welcome distraction."

"Ha! What am I distracting you from?"

"At the moment, numbers." He groaned a little and shook his head. "I'm supposed to be closing out the books for last month, but I'm having a hard time focusing."

"Wouldn't have anything to do with a certain blond resident, would it?" Grace gave him a knowing grin.

Brian laughed. "How do you know about that?"

"Krisi briefly mentioned it when we met last week. So how's it going between you two?"

"Good…" He paused for a moment. "It's going fine…actually, it's going great."

"But?"

Brian ran his fingers through his hair. "She doesn't seem to want to be seen in public together, not since the newspaper articles. It makes me wonder if she's embarrassed to be seen with me. Which then makes me wonder if our relationship is even real."

Grace leaned forward in her chair. "Have you talked to Krisi about it?"

He shook his head.

"It seems like a conversation you should have with *her*."

"Yeah, I suppose you're right."

"Brian, why haven't you told her your *real* role at The Athenian?"

He rubbed his hands over his face. "I don't know. I guess I just want to see how important money is to her. Does it really matter to her what I do or don't make?"

"I don't know," Grace said seriously. "But you need to be up front with her if you want your relationship to have a chance. After that, at least you'll know."

He let out a big breath. "Yeah, I suppose you're right. Again."

"I came by to let you know the rest of my furniture will be picked up on Friday. Laci's due back in a few weeks, and I want to make sure I have time to get the apartment cleaned so she can move her own furniture in."

Brian got all the pertinent information to make sure everything went smoothly when the movers arrived. After several more minutes of catching up and seeing how Hope's House,

Grace's shelter for abused women, was going, she left him to his numbers.

She'd given him a lot to think about. She was right, it was time to tell Krisi everything, then let the chips fall where they may.

Wednesday evening, Brian sat in Uncorked, waiting for Krisi. This was more public than most of their recent dates, and he was happy she'd agreed to it. Wednesday nights typically weren't busy at the wine bar, so Brian hoped they could have a quiet conversation without prying eyes.

Ten minutes after he arrived, Krisi walked in. His heart skipped a beat as he watched her make her way to him. He stood and pulled out her chair, but instead of sitting, she wrapped her arms around his neck and pulled his face down to hers.

"I've been thinking about this all day," she said, then stretched to press her lips to his. She lingered for a moment, but not nearly long enough, in his opinion.

He couldn't keep the grin off his face. At times like this, it seemed silly to question their budding relationship. He wrapped his arms around her waist and pulled her closer, loving the way she fit in his arms. It was like she was made for him, and he for her.

He pulled the seat out for her, then took his chair across the table. The bartender, Beau, came after they were settled.

"Good to see you two again." He smiled at them.

"Beau, good to see you. How're you enjoying Nashville?" Brian had learned the bartender recently moved here from Montana.

"I'm enjoying it. Melody has been great at helping me find my way around."

"Melody?" Krisi asked. "As in Melody Brews?"

Beau grinned and nodded. "I'm staying at her house. In Montana, I lived at a boarding house her sisters ran. Somehow, they talked me into joining them on a road trip to Nashville." He chuckled. "It's like living with three grandmothers. Melody seems to know every single woman within a hundred miles and thinks I need to meet them all." He chuckled. "Anyway, what can I get you two tonight?"

He took their order for wine and some small plates to share. In the center of the table, four wineglass charms, each with a different colored gem on them, surrounded a flickering candle. He brushed them aside and took her hand in his.

"How was your day today?" He loved the way her eyes sparkled in the candlelight.

She grinned. "Today was a big day. We ordered all the fixtures, shelving, and cabinetry for the shop. I can't wait for everything to arrive. It's going to look great in that space."

"I'm excited to have you there." He was looking forward to having the space filled with such a great company. He'd done some research after they'd talked about it, and from what he could find, her company did well. But even more than having the space filled, he was looking forward to having *her* around on a regular basis.

"Oh, and I booked a flight to Paris for Nikki and me. We need to visit the shop there. It sounds like there needs to be some personnel changes."

"Oh," he said. "You have to deal with that in person?"

"The joy of being the boss."

Beau was back and set a glass of white in front of Krisi and red in front of Brian. He placed the appetizers they'd ordered in the middle of the table. "Let me know if you two need anything else."

After Beau returned to the bar, Brian picked up the wine charm with the clear gem and held it out to her. "Would you like to decorate your glass?"

Krisi laughed. "I don't think we'll get our glasses confused, but sure." She took the charm from him and fastened it around the stem of her glass, then picked it up to admire the charm. "Now it's sparkly."

Brian tapped his glass to hers with a grin. He picked up her hand again and nodded to a ring she was wearing. "What kind of stone is this?"

It was a simple ring set on a white gold band. It had a few diamond chips on each side and a sparkling square-cut pale blue gem in the center. His interest in the ring was mostly an excuse to hold her hand, but looking at the glistening gemstone on her ring finger made him wonder what kind of a diamond Krisi would want. His heart lurched a bit in his chest at the thought. Why was he thinking about diamonds? And more specifically, why were diamonds and Krisi in the same thought?

Of course he knew why. Krisi had captured his heart. The real question was would she ever accept a ring from him?

"It's tourmaline," Krisi answered. "My grandmother gave me this ring. It's always been a favorite of mine. I love the shade of blue." She held her hand up and looked at the ring, oblivious to his wandering thoughts.

He wiped his sweaty palm on his jeans. When he reached for his wineglass, he realized his hand was shaky. He took a deep breath before picking it up.

"Hey, you okay? You look a little pale." Krisi's concerned voice cut through his thoughts.

He settled a smile on his face. "Yeah, I'm good."

He wasn't good. He could totally picture himself giving Krisi a ring. A diamond ring.

And it scared the heck out of him.

"So when do you leave for Paris?"

"On Friday. I..." She twirled her glass in her hand. "I was wondering if you'd like to come with me?" She dipped her head a little, her hair falling in front of her face, before she sat up straight and scooped her hair back.

"You want me to go to Paris with you?" Brian was stunned.

Her smile wobbled, and he realized she was nervous. "Yes, I'd love to show you around Paris. At least the parts I like, and you could meet my friends there."

Brian frowned, thinking about what it would take to leave The Athenian for any length of time. He didn't have anyone who could step in and manage the building if he went away. "That sounds amazing, Krisi..."

"I feel a *but* coming," she replied, her voice low.

He hoped what he had to say next wouldn't hurt her feelings or make her think he wasn't ready to level-up their relationship.

He blew out a breath and chose his words carefully. "As much as I'd love to go to Paris with you, I need more notice than a couple days." It killed him to say no, but at the same time, he wasn't sure he was ready for what a weekend in Paris would involve. Besides, his sister was home and he didn't want to run out on her. She'd just gotten here.

She frowned but nodded. "I understand. You probably need to ask for time off and all."

Brian took a deep breath. "Not exactly." Thinking about his conversation with Grace, he knew it was time to come clean. "So...you know how you've kept your ownership of Scent SCK a secret?" At her nod, he continued, "Well...I've kind of done the same thing."

Her brows furrowed together. "I'm not sure I understand?"

"Krisi, I don't *work* here at The Athenian...that's not true, I do work here. But..." He was fumbling, and by her confused expression, he could tell she had no idea where he was going. "I guess what I'm trying to say is, I work for myself. I *own* The Athenian."

Krisi sat quietly for several minutes, making his palms sweat again. He knew she was processing but couldn't tell how she felt about it.

"But...I have a lot of questions. I guess I mostly want to know why you felt you had to hide it from me?"

"It's not that I've hid it from you...or not *just* you. I've kept it from everyone. Except Shelby. She knows of course. And somehow Grace figured it out." This wasn't going well. He'd hoped it would ease her concern about the two of them, but instead, it felt like he was creating more distance between them.

"That last article in the *Daily* about us," Krisi said, "it mentioned some of your history. That you grew up in a lower-middle class family. Your parents died when you were a young adult. Did the reporter make all of that up?"

Brian shook his head and stared hard at his wineglass. "No, that was all true. We were a very normal middle class family. My parents worked hard and made a reasonable living, but we weren't 'well off' by any stretch of the imagination. And my parents did die," he said softly. "I was in the army when I got the call. They only reported part of the story. The reporter didn't do much digging." He looked up at her.

"I'm really sorry about your parents, Brian." She paused and took a sip of wine. "Do you want to share the rest of the story?"

He nodded. He hadn't shared the details of his life with anyone. It felt good that she wanted to hear them.

"When I graduated from high school, I had no idea what I wanted to do with my life. I knew college wasn't in my future, at least not immediately, so at eighteen, I joined the army. Shelby was only seven then." He was still sad about how much of Shelby's growing up he'd missed. "The weekend before I shipped out for bootcamp, I won the lottery."

Krisi's mouth dropped open. "Get out! Really?"

"Yeah, really. I'd never bought a lottery ticket before, but a buddy wanted to grab some tickets." He laughed at her expression. It probably mirrored his when he'd realized he won. "It was exciting, but it freaked me out. I knew I wasn't prepared to handle a huge sum of money, and I was only days away from boot-camp."

Krisi leaned forward, her eyes wide. "So what'd you do?"

"I hired a lawyer who was a good friend of my dad's, so I knew I could trust him. He claimed the money for me and, with the help of a financial adviser, invested it while I was in the military."

She leaned forward even more and lowered her voice. "Is it crass to ask how much?"

He grinned. "One hundred million dollars."

"What?" Krisi said loudly before lowering her voice again. "Really? How did you just walk away from that kind of money?"

"Well, I didn't exactly walk away. I just had to wait. Uncle Sam frowns on not showing up when you've committed. I used my time in the military to get a financial and business education. I read a ton of books, watched videos, and over the course of my enlistment, I developed a plan of what I wanted to do with the money when I got out. So no, I didn't walk away. I just got smart while it waited for me."

"Amazing." Krisi seemed genuinely awed, which made him smile. "How does The Athenian fit into this?"

He laughed. "One time while I was home on leave, I found this place. I was wandering around downtown and stumbled across an eyesore of a building." He looked around the bar, remembering the mess the building had been when he bought it. He'd seen beyond the mess. He'd been smitten at first sight, even when it didn't make sense. "It was in foreclosure and was a disaster. This was shortly after the market crashed and so much was in foreclosure. I fell in love with this building, even though it needed a lot of work. I let it sit for a few more years while I finished my time in the army. I figured out a plan for it but didn't want to start until my commitment was done. Each time I came home for a visit, I'd move a step closer. I hired an architect to draw up my vision. Found a contractor who could make it happen..."

He paused, knowing what was coming. The hardest time in his life.

"My time in the military was cut short by my parents' accident." Krisi reached across the table and put her hand over his. "They allowed me to be discharged early so I could take care of Shelby. She was still in high school, and I wanted her to finish and go to college. She's done amazing." He shook his head in wonder at his little sister. "Straight As in both high school and college, and she's only got one year to go. She'll be the first in our family to have a college degree." He knew he'd told her this before, but it felt like such a milestone for his family. Both he and Shelby had broken familial patterns—he in becoming an entrepreneur and Shelby in getting her degree.

Krisi's eyes were glistening in the candlelight, and she squeezed his hand. "That's amazing, Brian, that you would pivot your whole life to help your sister."

"You've got younger siblings. Wouldn't you do the same?" It didn't feel like anything extraordinary to keep Shelby in school and be her guardian. She was his family. His *whole* family.

Krisi nodded slowly. "Yeah...I guess I would. Lily's the same age as Shelby." She was quiet for a moment. "I can't imagine what you two went through. No wonder you're so close."

"Yeah, she's it for me. She's my family."

"You've done an amazing job with her, Brian. She's a great person."

"Well, thankfully, my parents did the hard part. She was already a great person when I took over. While Shelby finished high school, we stayed in our parents' house and kept as much the same as we could. It made the loss a little easier for both of us. But since I'd already met with an architect and had plans drawn up, it was just a matter of moving up the timeline with the contractor. And that's how The Athenian became one of the premier apartment buildings downtown."

"So..." Krisi looked around the wine bar. "This is all yours?"

He nodded. "It is. I held off doing anything with this floor until last year. I knew I wanted retail down here, so I culled through a lot of potential businesses to find the ones I felt were the right fit." He grinned at her. "I'm glad you're going to take over that last space. You'll do well there, I think."

Krisi smiled at him. "Thank you for sharing all that with me. I like getting to know you better."

"Can I ask you a question?" Brian was hesitant but needed to know her answer.

"Sure, anything."

"Are you embarrassed to be seen in public with me? Is that why we've been hiding out on the roof and in our apartments?"

Her eyes went wide at his question. "Oh, Brian. Is that what you think?" She let out a big breath. "I'm so sorry that's the impression I gave. Absolutely one hundred percent, *no,* I'm not embarrassed to be seen with you. I just didn't want our relationship splashed all over the papers. After years of having my dating life in the tabloids, I wanted *this* relationship to be just for me. For us. Are you sure you can't come to Paris with me?"

Brian felt the tension in his chest release. As much as he'd like to go to Paris, he had obligations here that needed to be dealt with. Namely, Shelby and The Athenian.

Chapter 15

KRISI

Three wishes:

- *Survive the family dinner*

- *Safe travels to Paris*

- *I hope Brian misses me while I'm gone*

E ARLY THE NEXT MORNING, Krisi sat at
the kitchen table, sipping her second cup

of coffee. Her father had woken her with another early morning phone call. She was getting tired of his calls ruining her sleep.

And now she was expected to show up for dinner the next night. She wasn't happy about having to delay her trip to Paris, but her father wouldn't take no for an answer. Geesh, she really needed to work on her boundaries with her father. Scratching out a note for Nikki to change their flight, Krisi swirled her coffee, debating whether to have another cup.

"You're becoming an early bird." Nikki walked into the kitchen and tossed a copy of the *Nashville Daily* in front of Krisi.

Since the first article had appeared, Nikki had gotten in the habit of picking up a copy of the paper each morning before coming to the apartment.

"Yes, another wake-up call from Daddy." She rolled her eyes and flipped through the paper in front of her. She stopped when she got to the society page and almost started laughing.

Nikki sat down next to her with a cup of coffee and looked at the pictures Krisi was staring at. "Hmm, something you want to share?"

The headline read *Wedding Bells for the Princess?* Two pictures of her and Brian from the evening before accompanied the short article. The first was of Brian handing her the wine glass charm, except the picture made it look like he was handing her a ring. The stone on the charm sparkled, and she suspected some photo doctoring had taken place to put the gem on the top of the ring instead of dangling to the side. The second picture was of Brian holding her hand and looking at her tourmaline ring. Again, it appeared some image tampering had taken place to make it look like her left hand instead of her right.

Krisi let out a huff. "No wonder Daddy woke me up this morning." She shook her head and explained what had really happened.

"So no wedding bells for the princess?" Nikki laughed.

"Princess. Heiress. Just once, I wish they'd use my name. But no. No wedding bells." Now that she had the image of Brian giving her a ring, she couldn't shake it. It surprised her how disappointed she felt it hadn't happened the way the newspaper portrayed. "Daddy's so upset about it, he insisted I come for a family dinner tonight."

"Tonight?"

Krisi nodded. "Do you mind calling and letting the pilot know we'll be delayed a few hours? We will still go, it'll just be later."

Nikki nodded. "Sure, no problem. Anything else you need to change before the trip?"

They talked about the schedule they'd set up for the next few days and made a few tweaks where they were needed.

"I'll pack your bag today. Anything in particular you want to wear?"

They wound up taking their coffee into her closet to make the necessary choices based on appointments and meetings. She loved Paris and looked forward to being back in the city.

"I invited Brian to come with us," she said softly.

"Oh. Wow."

"He can't come." Krisi pouted.

Nikki looked at her. "You're disappointed."

"Yeah," Krisi said. "I asked him on a whim, but now I'm really disappointed he can't make it."

"Too soon?" Nikki asked.

Krisi shrugged. "He said he needed more lead time, he couldn't just take off at the spur of the moment."

"Then find out how long he needs and ask again."

Nikki was so sensible sometimes, it was annoying. Why hadn't she thought of that?

They spent the rest of the day wrapping up loose ends, confirming appointments in Paris, and finishing her packing. The driver was scheduled to pick up Krisi at her apartment, along with her luggage, and take her to her parents' house. Nikki would be picked up before the driver came back for Krisi after dinner. Then they'd be on their way to the airport.

Dinner at the St. Claire house was always formal. For that reason, Krisi dressed with care. It was critical to select the appropriate outfit for the evening. Growing up, she'd learned the importance of dressing well, that it was, in her mother's opinion, a form of good manners. Wanting to be comfortable as well as stylish, she settled on a fitted black pantsuit with a white blouse and paired it with the diamond tennis bracelet she'd been given for her thirteenth birthday. With a spritz of her signature scent to boost her confidence, she headed out the door, trying to shake the feeling of heading to the gallows.

"Hey there." Krisi poked her head into Brian's office on her way out. By the immediate grin and intense look in his eyes, she knew she'd made the right decision to stop.

He stood and walked over to her. "So you're off to Paris?" He reached up and tucked a stray hair behind her ear.

"Dinner with the family first, then Paris. I wanted to ask you a question before I leave." She quickly added, "I don't need an answer right now, but I'd like for you to think about it."

She wished Brian could come with her tonight, but she wasn't ready to subject him to her family. More specifically, to her parents.

"Sure, what's up?"

She looped her arms around his neck. "If I were to invite you to Paris at a later date, how much time would you need to make arrangements?" Unable to resist the temptation, she raised up on her tippy-toes and pressed her lips to his.

Brian automatically wrapped his arms around her waist and pulled her closer. One hand was firm on her lower back and the other slid along her spine, sending shivers up and down it. What was intended to be quick kiss on her way out, turned into something she could get lost in.

She already missed him, and she hadn't even set a foot out of the building.

All too soon, he pulled back and leaned his forehead against hers while they both caught their breath.

"You're making it hard to say goodbye." His voice was raspy with desire.

Krisi felt her phone buzz, indicating her driver had arrived.

"My car is here." She laid her hand on his cheek and gazed into his eyes. "I'm going to miss you, but I'll be back in a few days."

"Two weeks," he said, then chuckled at her confused expression. "That's how long I need right now before we can go to Paris. But I'm working on reducing it."

She beamed. He *did* want to go to Paris with her.

"Travel safe." He unwrapped his arms and took a step back, leaving her feeling chilly. "Maybe you can figure out where you want to take me when we go to Paris together."

"I'll do that." Krisi gave him a quick peck on the lips. "Send me a picture of the sunrise tomorrow."

"Count on it." He grinned.

"I'll miss you." She started to back away.

"I'll miss you too." He shoved his hands in his pockets.

After a last look, she turned and walked out the lobby doors to meet her driver.

"Good evening, Greg." She waited until he opened the door, then slid into the back seat.

"Good evening, ma'am." He swung the door shut with a solid thump before circling around to climb in behind the wheel.

The car pulled away from the curb and weaved its way through traffic. Her sense of unease grew as the tall buildings faded behind her, replaced by the rolling hills of Belle Meade. Before she was ready, the car turned off the street and headed down the long, familiar driveway. It came to a stop in front of the home she'd only recently moved out of.

Greg opened her door, and she stepped out. She stood and stared up at the massive house where she'd grown up. As she approached the front door, it swung open, and she was greeted by their longtime butler, Harold.

"Miss Kristine." His tone was solemn, and he gave her a slight nod. "Your family is already in the dining room."

"Thank you, Harold." The door shut quietly behind her, and her heels echoed off the marble floor.

All four of her family members were seated in the formal dining room when she entered. Harold, who had followed her, pulled out her chair. Lily grinned from across the table, and Alex gave her a curious look. The expressions on their faces, combined with the empty chair to her right, raised a warning flag in her mind.

Her mother, seated at one end of the table next to the empty chair, ignored her arrival. At least her father, seated opposite her mother at the head of the table, acknowledged her with a dip of his chin.

All in all, a fairly normal start to what would no doubt be a very long evening.

Harold returned a few minutes later with a bottle of champagne and held it for her father to examine the label. On receiving his nod of approval, the cork was popped and sparkling wine was poured in each glass.

The longtime butler then stood rigidly at the corner of the table. "For the amuse-bouche, we have a fresh caught oyster served with a champagne mignonette. We've paired it with a blanc de blancs champagne. Enjoy."

He bowed slightly and backed away to make room for the servers. A small plate with a glistening oyster nestled on a half shell and topped with a vibrant green sauce was placed in front of each of them.

Oysters were Krisi's favorite, and she loved this appetizer. Their chef always found the freshest available. Her tongue delighted in the contrast between tangy mignonette, fresh salty oyster, and cool crisp champagne. Perfection in a single bite.

She sat back, enjoying the moment, thinking maybe this evening wouldn't be too horrible.

Unfortunately, her contentment was short-lived.

Harold stepped back into the dining room to announce a new arrival in that stuffy way of his. "Senator Black, sir."

The senator walked past the butler as if he wasn't there.

"Sorry I'm late, Robert. Got held up in a committee meeting." He moved to the head of the table and shook her father's hand, then turned to nod to Alex. "Alexander, always good to see you."

The empty chair suddenly made sense.

Why would Daddy invite the senator to a family dinner?

She dreaded the answer, and now, the appetizer she'd enjoyed moments before felt like a rock in her stomach.

This was definitely going to be a long meal.

The senator walked over to the other end of the table and held out his hand.

"Mrs. St. Claire, a pleasure to see you again." Instead of shaking her hand, he enveloped it in both of his and bent over, like he was greeting royalty.

Her mother tittered and might've even blushed.

Pleased with himself, the senator's chest puffed out a bit before he finally settled in the seat next to Krisi. He turned to her, lifted her hand from the table, and brought it to his lips, as if to kiss her knuckles. "Always a pleasure to see you, my dear."

She managed to wiggle her hand from his grasp a fraction of a second before his lips touched it. She looked at him and felt her upper lip curl before she smoothed her facial expression.

"I don't think we're at the hand kissing stage, Senator." She stifled the urge to dash to the bathroom to wash her hands and instead folded them in her lap.

Her father's glare sliced through her before he shifted his gaze to the senator. "Glad to have you join us, Michael. You're just in time for the first course."

With that, Harold reappeared with a bottle of Chablis for her father's approval. At his nod, he poured a glass for her mother, Krisi, and Lily before doing the same for the men at the table.

Harold resumed his position at one corner of the table for his next announcement. "For the first course, we have seared scallops on a bed of pureed organic cauliflower with a drizzle of truffle oil. We've paired it with a light-bodied Chablis. Enjoy."

As before, servers appeared and set a plate before each of them.

While Krisi might not have enjoyed the stifling atmosphere at these meals, the food was always top notch. Taking a deep breath to settle her stomach, she cut into a golden scallop and brought it to her mouth. The rich, earthy aroma of the truffle oil and the briny scent of the scallop made her mouth water. The caramelized sweetness of the scallop mixed with the creamy, buttery cauliflower and the luxurious hint of truffle was divine.

"Tell me, Senator, what brings you to our table tonight?"

Thank goodness Alex asked the question, because Krisi knew she couldn't. She sent him a brief, grateful look, then turned to the senator to hear his response.

Black flashed Alex a classic politician's smile—wide and insincere. "When your father extended the invitation, I couldn't resist. Not only do I get a delicious meal, but I get to spend time with all of you." His gaze lingered on Krisi. "I felt it was time to get to know you better."

The senator's intention to get to know her better didn't sit well with Krisi, and she chose to ignore it. Based on her sister's startled expression, Lily didn't think much of the comment either.

Conversation continued through dinner, and she did her best to stay out of it. Unless asked a direct question, she focused on the food in front of her. Despite Krisi giving every indication she wasn't interested in the senator, his lingering glances continued. He even started referring to her as *darling*.

Until tonight, she'd always loved lobster bisque, but now it sat heavy in her stomach. By the time the main course of beef Wellington, potatoes, and verts was served, her stomach was queasy and she struggled to eat. Sitting next to the senator was wreaking havoc with her nerves.

Krisi suffered through another hour, watching the senator guzzle her father's expensive wine and listening to him talk, making off-hand references to a relationship between the two of them that didn't—and wouldn't!—exist.

She had no idea what was going on between him and her father, but she felt like a pawn in the game they were playing. A game only the two of them were aware of or knew the rules to.

Krisi had no desire to be part of any of it. All she wanted was to be with Brian.

As the servers cleared the plates from a small, fresh salad served after the main course, Krisi was startled to feel a hand sliding up her thigh.

"What the...?" Disgusted, she abruptly pushed her chair back.

The senator grimaced when his hand became trapped beneath the arm of the chair, and his conversation with her mother came to an abrupt halt. He wrestled his arm free and glared at her as he rubbed his forearm.

"What did you do that for?" His words were slurred, his voice too loud for the dinner table.

"For some reason I cannot fathom, Senator, your hand was on my leg." She stood and dropped her napkin onto her plate. "You should keep better track of where your hands are." She turned to her father. "Excuse me."

It took everything in her not to run from the dining room and straight out the front door. Instead, she walked slowly with her head held high. At least until she was out of sight. Then, she picked up her pace and hurried to the downstairs half bath. She was reaching for the doorknob as her sister walked out.

Lily gave her a questioning look. "What's going on between you and Senator Black?"

Krisi glanced back at the dining room, then leaned closer to Lily. "Nothing," she said in a harsh whisper. "That man is making me so mad. He just tried to feel me up, right in the middle of a conversation with Mother!"

Lily's hand flew to her mouth, and her face contorted in disgust. "Yuck! Why is he trying to make it sound like you two are an item already?"

"I have no idea, but I can assure you we're not" Krisi checked they were still alone. "He's creeping me out. I really do *not* want to go back in there and sit next to him."

"Ugh. I don't blame you. I've always had weird vibes from him too, but he's never tried anything like that." Lily shuddered. "Why don't you hide out in the powder room for a few minutes?"

Krisi watched her sister disappear into the dining room, then stepped into the small bathroom and locked the door. She put the toilet seat down, plopped down on it, and took a few deep breaths. Returning to the table was the last thing she wanted, but it was expected of her. She would give herself as much time as she needed to calm her nerves and settle her mind.

She jumped at a sudden knock on the door.

"Kristine, darling?"

Her skin crawled at the sound of her name coming out of the senator's mouth.

"I just wanted to make sure you're okay."

"Thank you, Senator. I'm fine." She took another deep breath and released it. "I'll be out in a minute."

She took her sweet time touching up her makeup, fixing her hair, washing her hands. Then she put her ear to the door. Not hearing anything, she turned the knob, slowly opened the door, and stepped out. As it swung shut behind her, she turned to find Senator Black standing there.

"Oh!" Krisi's hand flew to her heart, now thumping double-time. "You startled me."

She turned toward the dining room, but before she could take a step, his clammy fingers tightened around her wrist, and he jerked her around to face him.

"Do not walk away from me." His eyes narrowed.

Krisi looked at her wrist and twisted it free of his grasp. "Senator, I am going back to the table." She rubbed her wrist. "I suggest you do the same."

She made the mistake of turning her back to him. He grabbed her forearm and yanked. Her back slammed against the door, her head bouncing off the wood. Pain pulsed through her body, and stars danced in front of her eyes.

Krisi couldn't catch enough breath to cry out.

He slapped his hands against the door on either side of her head, and pushed his body against hers, his weight holding her in place.

"I said"—his breath smelled of wine, and she turned her face to the side—"Don't. Walk. Away. From me."

He released her jaw, dragged his fingertips down the side of her face, then his long fingers circled her neck.

This man was unhinged.

Krisi was terrified. She shivered and choked out a cough, wishing Brian was there.

No. I cannot show fear. She needed to face him on her own.

"Take your hands off me." She focused on keeping the quiver from her voice. "Now."

Light from the chandelier overhead glinted in his eyes.

"And if I don't?" His eyebrow lifted, and his tone was taunting. "Your doorman isn't here to rescue you, Kristine. It's just you and me." With each word, he squeezed her neck a little tighter.

The senator leaned closer, placed his mouth against the side of her neck, and dragged his lips across her skin.

Her eyes squeezed shut, and disgust shuddered through her.

"Mmm, you like that, don't you?" His words vibrated against her.

Behind him, Alex appeared from the dining room. He stopped short and, his eyes wide with anger, started forward.

Krisi gave a slight shake of her head. *Video*. She mouthed the word, so as not to alert the senator to his presence.

Alex quietly slipped his cell phone from his pocket, held it up, and began recording.

"Senator," Krisi said loud enough for her voice to be heard. "You need to get off me and leave me alone."

"You don't seem to understand what's going on here, Kristine." His tongue snaked out to touch her skin, then he lifted his head and looked her in the eyes. "You are *mine*."

"No, I am not, Senator." She lifted her chin and stiffened her spine. "We do not have a relationship. We never have, and we *never* will."

"That's where you're wrong, Kristine. I *own* you." His smile turned even more sinister. "I can do whatever I want to you. Tonight, I will take you home with me. I have dreamed of this night for so long. I have very special plans for you."

His words sent a shiver of fear through her body. It took everything in her to not look at her brother, standing just a few feet away. She knew he wanted to help her and was probably frustrated she'd held him off. But she also knew, without the video evidence, no one would believe how unhinged and dangerous the senator was.

"Senator, you don't love me." The thought made her nauseous. "Because this is not how you treat someone you love."

His thin fingers wound around her neck again.

"Love?" He spat out a harsh laugh. Spittle landed on her cheek, making her cringe. "I never said *anything* about love, Kristine. I said I *own* you, not that I love you." His voice was louder. "You are what is called a sacrificial lamb, my dear."

Confusion added to her fear. "I have no idea what you're talking about, Senator." She tried to wriggle free. "You're hurting me and starting to scare me."

"I'm scaring you, am I? Good. I want you scared. I want you to *plead* with me." His eyes were unfocused, like he was looking at something or someone not there. His fingers started tightening around her neck again.

"Sen—"

She squeaked when his grip tightened. Breathing became difficult. Her heartbeat pounded in her ears. The light began to dim.

Instinct took over and muscle memory from the self-defense class she'd taken a few months earlier kicked in. She brought her knee up hard between his legs.

The senator's eyes were wide as saucers when he released her neck. A high-pitched squeal came from his mouth, and he stumbled back a step.

Krisi reached up, grabbed his ears, and yanked his head down. There was a loud crunch when the senator's nose made contact with her knee. Blood poured from his broken nose and dripped onto his starched, white shirt. His hands flew up to protect his face, and he started to straighten. Krisi shoved him before he could regain his composure. His heel slipped on the marble floor, and his arms windmilled. He landed on his rear end, but momentum flipped him back, and his head hit the floor with a sickening thud.

She ran to Alex, who stood with his mouth open, his eyes wide as he continued filming.

Lily and their parents rushed through the doorway. Face pale, eyes wide, her father stared at the sight of a Tennessee senator curled up in a ball, holding his nose, getting blood all over their expensive, imported marble floor.

"I'll call 911." Lily stepped around the senator, giving a wide berth, and used the phone on a nearby table.

"I don't know who taught you self-defense, but we owe them a lot right now." Alex put his arm around Krisi's shoulders and pulled her close. "You were magnificent."

She leaned against him, allowing her body to relax, just a bit, and was grateful for his warmth and strength. Now was not the time to collapse. Later, she could think about what had happened.

After a few minutes, there was an aggressive knock on the door, and they all jumped.

"I'll get it." Lily rushed to open the door.

"We received a call about an altercation at this address." Two police officers stood at the door, their badges shining in the porch lights.

"Come in." Lily stepped aside to allow them entry.

The older of the two officers squatted next to the senator, then spoke into the radio attached to the shoulder of his uniform. He reached down to check his pulse, and the senator's arm lashed out, grabbing a handful of the policeman's shirt.

"Get off me," he growled. Something had surely snapped in his brain. His feral gaze raced around the room until it landed on Krisi. "I'm going to destroy you and that doorman boyfriend of yours."

"You're the one who will be destroyed, Senator." Krisi didn't back down; she returned his glare with her own.

"You *can't* destroy me." He laughed maniacally. "I own you, little girl. I own you and your pathetic father and all of this." He waved his hand around, as if to imply he owned their home.

This couldn't be. Krisi's heart leapt in her chest. As soon as he was gone, she needed to find out what was happening.

"Relax, Senator." The officer pulled the hand away from his shirt.

The senator was still making threats when the other officer separated Krisi from the group to take her statement. Krisi related what happened, showed her the bruises on her wrists and the blood on her hands from when she pushed him away.

By the time the police had finished recording everyone's statements and led the senator out of the house, Krisi was exhausted and ready to leave. She looked at her father, who was staring at the blood pooled where the senator had been.

"You and I need to have a conversation, Father." She was owed answers. "What the heck did that lunatic mean when he said he *owned* you and me?"

"Who's the doorman?" Her father evaded her question with one of his own.

Krisi shook her head, knowing she would get nowhere with him tonight.

"I'll tell you all about him later." She was much too drained to deal with this right now. "I have to go. I have a plane waiting for me."

Krisi strode out of the house and slid into the backseat of the waiting car. Her head fell back on the leather seat, and with a heavy sigh, she closed her eyes She was grateful to be leaving this mess behind. At least for a few days.

Chapter 16

BRIAN

SUNRISE ON THE ROOF was lonely. Brian sat on a stool, staring at the impressive sky in front of him, but he was having a hard time enjoying it. Krisi was in Paris and would be for the next few days. Shelby was sleeping in, since her shift at the wine bar kept her up late. He smiled, thinking about his and Krisi's last conversation. She'd asked him to pick a date for them to go to Paris.

He'd stayed awake most of the night thinking about that. It was a weighty invitation. Could he fit into her world? He was working class regardless of his bank account. Sure, he owned a luxury apartment building, but he worked for a living. Could he be comfortable in a world where people flitted off to parts around the globe? He realized as soon as the thought formed, it was unfair to Krisi. She was in Paris for work, not *flitting off* on a whim. She worked as hard as he did, just differently.

What would it be like if he hired a manager at The Athenian? It would certainly give him some free time to explore other options. Like a relationship with Krisi. As uncomfortable as the idea of hiring someone to do his job was, he knew it was important to step out from behind the doorman-manager facade and step into being the businessman he hid from the world.

Was he ready?

There was a lot he needed to think about before Krisi returned. He stared at the horizon, not seeing the colors painted across the sky, while he finished his coffee. When the cup was empty, he returned to his apartment to find Shelby at the kitchen counter.

"You're up early." He ruffled her hair as he walked past her.

"You're smiling, so I'm guessing you haven't read today's *Daily* yet?"

He turned back to her and sat next to her at the counter. "No, should I?"

"I'm not sure, to be honest. So far, everything they've printed has been wrong, so there's no reason to think this is different." She set the paper in front of him and slowly he turned the pages until he landed on the article in question.

Right Bride, Wrong Groom

Kristine St. Claire, daughter of Robert St. Claire, is indeed engaged, but not to Brian Streatt, the doorman at The Athenian, as last reported. Instead, Ms. St. Claire is engaged to Senator Michael Black, one of the most powerful men at the Tennessee state capital. Just last evening, the happy couple celebrated their engagement at a family dinner at the St. Claire mansion.

The bride-to-be flitted off to Paris,
no doubt in search of the perfect
wedding dress.

The article was accompanied by a somewhat grainy image of Krisi and the senator
dancing. The senator held her close and appeared to be whispering in her ear. It wasn't a
good picture of either of them.

Even though he knew the article—and picture—was a complete fabrication, the words
and image made his stomach churn.

"Hey, you okay?"

He'd forgotten his sister was sitting next to
him and was startled when she laid her hand
on his arm.

"Yeah," he said unconvincingly. "I'll catch
up with Krisi later and let her know what the
paper is saying."

Although now that he thought about it,
he wasn't sure he wanted to bother her with
it. A small, unacknowledged part of him was
concerned the article might be true. He stood
up and feigned indifference. "I'm off to grab a
shower and get my day going."

Shelby narrowed her eyes at him but didn't say anything. He could feel her stare all the way to his room. When he closed the door, he slumped onto the bed and picked up his phone. Should he text her? No, he decided. Instead, he would google to see if she happened to be in the Paris papers. If she actually *was* wedding dress shopping, it would be news over there, wouldn't it?

His search did nothing to calm his tense nerves, though nothing current came up about her in Paris. He tossed his phone on the bed and headed into the bathroom for a shower, contemplating whether to reach out to Krisi. He hated to bother her with this newest article. He wasn't so insecure he needed her to reassure him. Was he? He wasn't actually sure, which was frustrating. This was new territory for him.

He needed to figure out what he knew to be true. Krisi hadn't mentioned anything about dinner with the senator. In fact, she'd asked *him* to go to Paris with her. He couldn't wait to explore Paris with the woman he loved. That thought gave him pause. Since his parents' deaths, he hadn't allowed himself a serious relationship. His sole concern had been Shelby. *Did* he love Krisi? He stood under the shower, waiting for the excuses to come. All the reasons he couldn't, or shouldn't, be in love with Krisi. Instead, he felt calm. Content. Happy.

He'd never expected to fall in love. Especially not with someone like Krisi. An heiress. But she was exactly who he'd fallen in love with. Her kindness, generosity, and humor weren't seen by the press, or at least they didn't report on them. She wasn't a snob. She was real. And fun. And a hard worker. He admired what she was doing with Grace for abused women. The fact that she had four stores around the world that were all doing amazingly well was a testament to her business acuity.

Feeling better, he turned off the water, toweled dry, and put on his work uniform. Today's version included a lime-green vest. Minutes later, he headed out the door with a clearer head and better attitude. If he was going to hire a manager for The Athenian, he needed to come up with a list of job responsibilities. He liked having something positive to think about and work toward.

He walked down the back stairs, into his office, and opened the door to the lobby. Sitting behind his desk, he picked up his phone and typed out a text to Krisi.

BRIAN: Hey, how's Paris?

KRISI: ...

Brian smiled at the three little dots on the screen. He'd missed seeing and talking with her this morning.

KRISI:

KRISI: ...

KRISI:

Brian sat for several minutes staring at his phone, waiting, but nothing further popped up on the screen. Confused, he set the phone aside. He knew Krisi was working in Paris and consoled himself by remembering she was probably being pulled in several directions. He'd hear from her at some point. In the meantime, he had his own work to get to.

He opened a folder on the corner of his desk. He called it his *one day* folder. In it, he stuck ideas that came up and he'd think *one day, I'd like to do that.* The folder had grown over the years because he never had time for new projects. The Athenian took all his time.

Which brought his thoughts back to hiring a manager. He spent the day figuring out what the role might be. He wasn't prepared to give up the financial side of the job, but there were a lot of tasks that could be taken off his plate. By the end of the morning, he had the role mapped out and was ready to post the position and start the interview process. Since his military days, having a plan had brought him comfort. The idea of having an open schedule was thrilling but intimidating.

Routine had ruled his life for a long time. Every day in his military career had been mapped out. When he returned home to take care of Shelby, all those years ago, creating and sticking to a routine had been crucial. In the early days, his grief had almost overwhelmed him, and he'd floundered. He remembered the day a buddy from his unit visited. His friend hadn't known it, but he'd saved Brian from spiraling out of control. He'd offhandedly recommended Brian create a routine, like they'd had in the military. It had taken him a few weeks, but it brought a lot of comfort and stability to his life at a time when he desperately needed it. Somehow, the routines had stayed.

After finishing up in his office, he spent some time looking at his calendar for the next few months to map out what the timeframe might look like to hire and train someone, so he could take some time to travel with Krisi. The idea of exploring Paris with her appealed to him. It was fun to go down the rabbit holes of where he'd like to visit.

He wouldn't let himself believe the article. It couldn't be true. He *knew* how they felt about each other, and no article in the *Daily* could convince him otherwise.

The following morning, Brian still hadn't heard from Krisi. He took his phone to the roof and decided to text her a sunrise picture.

BRIAN: Sunrise in Nashville's not the same without you. Miss you

KRISI: ...

The dots disappeared again. And nothing.

He wasn't sure what to make of her silence. It was late morning in Paris, so she was probably knee-deep in meetings.

By the third day with no communication from her, Brian was beginning to question everything. He was ready to see her in person and stop all the scenarios going through his mind.

BRIAN: Are you heading back today? I can't wait to see you

KRISI: Brian, I need you to stop texting me. Didn't you see that I'm engaged to Senator Black? It's inappropriate for you to continue bothering me.

Brian recoiled, as if he'd been physically struck. He stared at the phone in disbelief, willing her to call him so they could talk this through, so he could understand what was going on.

Something wasn't right.

Maybe if he heard the words from her mouth, he would believe it.

Maybe.

After starting and erasing several messages, he tossed his phone aside and walked out of his bedroom. If she didn't want to hear from him, he had to respect it. He'd see her when she got back to Nashville.

Hopefully.

His mind wandered to the article about Krisi and Senator Black's engagement. She'd just confirmed his greatest fear. She *really* was engaged. Even though, just a couple of days earlier, she'd invited him to go to Paris with her.

Nothing made sense.

"Morning," he said to Shelby as he walked past her on his way to the kitchen.

Shelby looked up from her phone and immediately set it face down on the counter. "You okay? You don't look so good."

"Thanks a lot." He tried to make a joke of it, but it landed flat. He nodded to her phone, curious why she'd flipped it over so quickly. "Whatcha lookin' at?"

"Oh, nothing. Just scrolling. You know."

She wouldn't meet his eyes, and he knew her well enough to know she was hiding something.

"Shelb, what's going on?"

She took a deep breath, flipped the phone over, and slid it to him.

He picked it up and immediately felt his heart clench. There, on whatever social media platform his sister had been scrolling, was a picture of Krisi, sitting on a chaise longue in a bridal boutique.

She looked stunning, surrounded by wedding gowns, and she held a bottle of her perfume. He could feel the blood drain from his face, and the phone slipped from his hand onto the countertop.

So it was true.

She really was engaged to the senator.

And she was in Paris to find a bridal gown.

He slid the phone across the counter back to Shelby, then stood and walked out the door to the elevator.

"Wait, Brian—"

He heard Shelby calling from the apartment, but he didn't turn back.

He had no idea where he was going, but he knew he needed fresh air. The roof held too many memories with Krisi, so he pushed the down button, and as soon as the doors opened, he headed across the lobby to the front doors.

His mood plummeted even further when he stopped in front of the empty storefront that was set to house Krisi's boutique. He wondered if it would still happen. They had a signed contract, but would she want to open her shop here if she were married to Senator Black?

And would he want to force her to go through with it? Seeing her everyday would be torture if she was married to Black.

Sullenly, he turned and walked down the hallway, past the bookshop, past the spa, and made his way into Melody Brews instead of out the door. He walked past his normal spot by the door and sat at a small table in the back corner. If memory served, this was where Krisi had been sitting shortly after she moved in. The day he invited her to watch the sunrise with him.

He slumped into the chair and rubbed his hands over his face. Melody set a piping hot cup of coffee in front of him.

"Morning." She looked at him with concern. "You okay?"

He nodded and gave her a quiet "Yeah." At her questioning look, he shook his head. "No, I'm not okay."

"You want company?"

Brian thought about it for a moment. Did he want company? Melody was a good listener, but was he ready to talk about everything? He shrugged and motioned to the chair across from him.

"So what's happened to make you so blue?" she asked. "Is it because Krisi's out of town?"

Melody always seemed to know everything that was going on in The Athenian. Even more than he did, some days.

"Well, yes and no." He took a sip of coffee to settle his mind. "Two days ago, the day after Krisi left for Paris, the *Nashville Daily* reported she and Senator Black were engaged."

"*Engaged?* To Senator Black?" Melody's face showed she hadn't seen the article. "Oh, I can't believe she wants to marry that toad. And nothing that rag prints is true...you know that, Brian."

Her comments made him feel a little lighter. It wasn't just him who thought Krisi would never marry that man. "That's what I thought initially."

She leaned forward and narrowed her eyes a bit. "So what's changed your mind?"

"Well...Krisi." He pulled out his phone and showed her the text.

Melody's eyebrows shot up into her graying hair. "Oh, I just can't believe that. It doesn't even sound like how she talks." She dismissed the text. "Besides, I've seen the way she looks at you, Brian. That woman is in love...and *not* with the senator."

"That's what I thought too." He opened the social media site Shelby had been on and searched her name to find the image of Krisi surrounded by wedding gowns. "But it looks like she's shopping for a wedding dress, after all."

He felt the heavy weight of reality weigh on his heart. He recognized this feeling in his body. It was a different rendition of grief. His heart felt torn apart.

Again.

A customer walked in, and Melody called, "I'll be right there." She handed the phone back to Brian, then patted his hand. "Did you read the caption on that post?"

He shook his head.

"You should. She'll be home soon, honey. Talk to her. It'll be all right."

He wasn't sure he wanted to read what was going on in the bridal boutique, but he nodded. "Thanks, Melody. I appreciate your comments."

"You'll see." She stood and walked to the counter to talk with the customer.

Brian couldn't imagine how this situation would be all right. He felt his future being ripped apart, similar to when his parents died. A deep unsettled feeling lodged in his heart. A future he hadn't even dared to dream was all of a sudden taken from him. By the least likely person.

He'd seen the way Krisi responded to Senator Black when he brought her to The Athenian. The man had frustrated her, and she hadn't appeared to be attracted to him in the least. What changed? Or was Melody right, and all of this was a crazy mix-up? How did that explain her text?

With a heavy heart, Brian gave Melody a halfhearted wave and decided a walk in the fresh air was still needed.

Chapter 17

KRISI

Three wishes:

- *Sunrise on the roof with Brian.*

- *A good conversation with Daddy.*

- *Senator Black out of my life for good.*

FRIDAY MORNING, KRISI STEPPED onto the plane at Paris-Le Bourget. The small airport was the easiest one to go through when she flew in and out of Paris. She dropped, exhausted, onto a soft leather seat. Relief coursed through to be headed home.

Home, she realized, wasn't the sprawling mansion where she'd grown up. *Home* was The Athenian.

More specifically, *home* was *Brian*. And since Brian was at The Athenian, that's where she wanted to be. Needed to be.

Krisi had missed him the past several days. She'd had her fair share of boyfriends, dates, whatever, over her life, but never before had she felt like half her heart was missing when they were apart. Work had kept her busy, and she was pleased with everything they'd accomplished during the short trip, but the aggravation of losing her phone had made the trip feel much longer.

She'd been able to use Nikki's phone for business calls, but she didn't have Brian's number memorized. She looked up the number for The Athenian, but every time she had a few spare minutes, the timing was off. She didn't want to call his office at three o'clock in the morning. He must be wondering why she'd been silent.

She thought back to a few days earlier when she'd stepped onto the plane after the family dinner. Her hand and shirt were splattered with blood, her clothes rumpled beyond repair, her throat and wrist bruised.

Nikki had been shocked and insisted she press charges against the senator. That was when she discovered her phone was missing. She used Nikki's phone to call the Nashville Police Department and started the process of filing a report with the promise to sign the paperwork as soon as she was back in Nashville.

Senator Black would not be happy to learn she was pressing charges. Neither, she guessed, would her father. Nikki had taken pictures of Krisi's bruises and texted them to the police officer before Krisi took a shower and changed into clean, comfortable clothes.

She'd also texted her sister to see if her phone had fallen out at her parents' house. Lily hadn't been able to find it, which led to the question, *where was her phone?* Maybe it had dropped out in the car on the way to the airport. She could deal with it when Greg picked up her and Nikki in a few hours.

Nikki plopped down in the seat across the aisle from her. "I am so ready to be back to Nashville." Krisi took a glass of water offered by the flight attendant and nodded her thanks.

"It was a good trip though, wasn't it? Getting your perfumes in all five *Say Oui* bridal boutiques is epic."

Krisi let Nikki ramble for twenty minutes, giving a rundown of their accomplishments over the week. She'd learned early in their friendship that Nikki liked to recap events as a way of processing and decompressing. So letting her run through the last few days was a good way for both of them to wind down.

Like Nikki said, it had been a very successful trip. Krisi had needed to make some management adjustments in her Paris shop, but she was pleased with how it turned out. The new manager would be a great asset to her business and was someone she could trust.

After Nikki wound down and they'd eaten a light breakfast, Krisi slept the remainder of the flight. It was early afternoon when they arrived in Nashville, and Krisi had taken a shower and changed into a fresh outfit before landing. As much as she wanted to go straight to The Athenian to see Brian, their first stop needed to be the police station.

Nikki had called the police officer working the case upon landing, and everything Krisi needed to sign had been printed out by the time they arrived. The officer took advantage of having Krisi there to pepper her with more questions about the timeline and actions that had taken place. Fortunately, Alexander had sent the video to the police, which answered a lot of their questions.

Rehashing the incident was difficult for Krisi. All the feelings she'd had to tamp down over the past week so she could focus on business were bubbling to the surface. She remembered the fear coursing through her when she realized Black couldn't be reasoned with, that the man was completely unhinged.

When she finished signing the paperwork and answering the officers' questions, Krisi and Nikki climbed into their waiting car and, finally, made their way to The Athenian.

Nerves fluttered in Krisi's stomach in anticipation of her reunion with Brian. As soon as the car parked in front of the building, Krisi rushed into the lobby. Disappointment settled over her when she found Brian's office door locked. A quick trip to the second floor was equally discouraging, with no answer at his apartment door.

Frustrated and let down, she made her way to the sixth floor to find Nikki settled on the couch in her living room.

"I didn't expect you to be here so quickly." Nikki looked up from the paper she was leafing through.

Krisi frowned. "Brian's not home. I wish I had my phone to call or text him."

"I've got the new one." She nodded to a box on top of a stack of mail on the coffee table. "But it won't help you right now." Nikki stopped flipping pages and stared, her mouth open, at the article in front of her. "Oh my golly!"

Krisi sat next to her and looked at the paper. Her eyes went wide when she read the short article declaring her engagement to Senator Black. She snatched the paper from Nikki's hands and flipped to the front page.

"This is from the day after we left. I can't believe he did this." She stood and threw the paper on the coffee table, then paced in front of it. "I wonder if Father knows about it." She stopped midpace to look at Nikki with wide eyes. "Oh no...what if Brian saw this? I can't imagine what he must be thinking."

Nikki looked at her watch. "We have the bachelor auction tonight. Do you want to visit your father before it?"

Krisi nodded. "Let me change, then we'll visit Daddy."

Krisi and Nikki stepped out of the elevator on the top floor of the St. Claire Industries building in downtown Nashville. Both her brother's and father's offices were housed on this floor, along with the other executive offices. Nikki took a seat in the lobby while Krisi continued down the hallway.

"Ms. St. Claire, a pleasure to see you." Her father's secretary looked anything but pleased to see her. "Do you have an appointment today?"

"Good to see you, Nadine. No, I didn't have time to make one. I just need to pop in for a few minutes."

"I'm sorry, but Mr. St. Claire has a full schedule today."

Krisi almost felt bad brushing past Nadine—the woman was only doing her job—but she was going to see her father and she was going to see him *now*. She strode down the thick-carpeted hallway to her father's office and tapped the door before letting herself in. Her father was in a discussion with another man, and they both looked up at her unexpected entrance.

"Kristine? Did Nadine not tell you I was in a meeting?" Her father's voice was even, but his eyes were narrow, glaring at her.

"She did, but I need a couple of minutes of your time." She turned to the other man. "I'm sorry to interrupt your meeting, Mr. Watkins, but can I borrow Daddy for a couple of minutes?" She'd met the older man many times at various events around town.

He smiled at her as he stood. "Of course. I'll go grab a cup of coffee."

She and her father watched him walk out of the room. As soon as the door closed, Krisi turned to face her father.

"I know your time is valuable, so I'll get right to the point. Did you see the article about my *engagement* to Senator Black?"

"I...engaged?"

His obvious confusion told Krisi all she needed to know. He hadn't been in on it.

"Yes. Apparently, after dinner the other night, someone told the *Nashville Daily* the senator and I are engaged. I'm wondering who would say such a thing. Especially since dinner didn't end well for the senator."

Her father sat heavily in his seat and motioned for her to sit in a chair across from him. She was wound up and would have preferred to pace, but she sat. She wanted to hear what he had to say. She crossed her ankles, settled her hands in her lap, and waited.

He spoke softly. "I didn't know he did that." He looked up at her, his voice still quiet. "Would it be so bad to be engaged to him? You wouldn't have to actually *marry* him."

Everything in her wanted to slam things around and yell at him, but looking at the broken man in front of her, she couldn't. She'd never seen her father look so old, so fragile.

"What's going on between you and Senator Black, Daddy? Friday night, before he left with the police, he said he *owned* you. He said he owned *me*. Why would he say that?"

Her father looked at his folded hands. "Senator Black is the head of the Future Technology and Innovation Committee at the capitol. The committee passes bills that directly affect our business. We worked together for seven years to get him onto that committee, and now he's the chairman, so he was able to introduce legislation to greatly benefit our business.

"And what did he want in exchange for getting the bill passed?" Krisi's heart beat faster while she waited for her father's response.

He looked up from his hands and into her eyes. "Initially, he said we'd work it out later, maybe stock shares or something."

"I'm guessing that's not where he landed?" Krisi raised an eyebrow.

He slowly shook his head. "After the bill passed, he said he wanted a stronger tie to our family and business."

Krisi's heart pounded in her ears; she knew what was coming.

"He said he wanted...you." Her father's voice was barely above a whisper.

She looked at him, stunned. She couldn't imagine her father ever agreeing to such a deal. She'd been ready to blast him but stopped at the look of regret in his eyes.

"And you thought that was a fair exchange?" She couldn't help the snark in her tone.

He shook his head. "No. I thought he just wanted to get to know you...you know, be seen around town with you, dance with you at the gala. Important men like to be seen with young, beautiful women."

She recalled their conversation a few weeks ago, the one that prompted her to move to her own space. He'd wanted her to spend time with the senator and get to know him. Now she understood why her father had asked it of her.

"Friday afternoon," he continued softly, looking at his clasped hands again, "he called and said he wanted a family dinner to announce your engagement." He looked up at her again. "He made it sound like you two were already getting along. To be honest, I wasn't thrilled by it. I knew you wouldn't be happy with someone like him. I didn't realize he hadn't even talked to you about it."

"I didn't think my happiness was part of the equation. What changed?"

"I guess I have. The more I've seen of Black, the less I want to be part of his world." He took a deep breath and let it out. "I guess...I was wrong to say marriages are made in the boardroom. That's what I learned from my father, but it didn't work out so great for me. I'd like marriage to be better for you. Of course your mother has given me three amazing children, so maybe it hasn't been all bad."

Tears pricked the corners of Krisi's eyes as she thought of all the miscommunication and misunderstanding of the last several weeks between them. For him to admit he was wrong about anything was shocking; for him to admit that maybe his marriage hadn't been a good choice was sad. She didn't want that for him anymore than she wanted it for herself.

"When I saw him with his hand around your neck..." His face paled as he looked at the yellow marks still showing there.

Krisi stood, walked around his desk, and stopped next to him. Needing the connection, she laid a hand on his arm. "Daddy, I'll be okay. My bruises will fade. But I want you to know I've already gone to the police station and filed a report. I hope there's nothing that can implicate you when he goes down. Because he *is* going down."

With tears in his eyes and relief on his face, her father stood and pulled her into a hug. Krisi couldn't remember the last time he'd hugged her. She breathed deeply, taking in the scent that was her father. Sandalwood and cardamom and hints of aged leather. It was this very scent that had started her love for creating perfumes.

He pulled back but kept his hands on her shoulders. "I support you, Krisi. He will not go down lightly and will sling a lot of dirt. Nothing will stick to me though." At her raised eyebrow, he continued, "I was careful in my dealings with him. Our lawyers looked over everything and made changes when needed." He nodded to her. "Go get him, honey. Take him down."

Chapter 18

BRIAN

BRIAN SAT IN THE greenroom, waiting for his turn in the bachelor auction, chatting with a football player and a hockey player he'd watched on television. It was comforting to see they were just as nervous about this event as he was. The idea of women *bidding* on him was unsettling. He was a nobody. He'd worked hard to keep a low profile in Nashville, and now he was "coming out," so to speak.

The door opened and the air shifted as Senator Michael Black walked in. He wore a tailored dark gray suit and a pale gray button-up shirt with his initials on the cuff. Diamond cufflinks glinted at his wrists beneath his jacket.

Brian intentionally turned away from the door and continued his conversation. The hairs on the back of his neck tingled when the senator stopped next to him.

"Gentlemen," Black said smoothly. He held out a hand to the football player. "Senator Michael Black, a pleasure to meet you." He then shook the hockey player's hand before turning to Brian and making a show of recognizing him. "My goodness, I remember you. From The Athenian, right?"

Brian nodded.

"Interesting choice to have a *doorman* as one of our bachelors. Mr. Streatt, isn't it?"

Brian nodded without bothering to extend his hand. He only stood and excused himself. He was not interested in having a conversation with the man who'd ruined any hope of a future with Krisi. He walked to the opposite side of the room, picked up a bottle of water from a table filled with food and drink, then walked out the door. He needed to put as much space as possible between himself and the senator. He shook his head. It was just his luck the senator was one of the bachelors.

He saw Grace backstage talking with another man and made his way toward her.

She looked up and smiled at him. "Oh Brian, have you met Alexander yet?" She introduced the tall dark-haired man next to her.

"No, I don't think...wait, you look familiar." Brian couldn't piece together where he might have seen this man, but he held out a hand. "Brian Streatt."

"Alex St. Claire." Alex smiled at him.

Clarity came immediately. He was Krisi's brother. "Of course," he said. "I saw you having a drink with Krisi at Uncorked not long ago."

"It's nice to finally meet you," Alex said with a grin. "Krisi's told me a lot about you. I think she got back into town this morning—have you seen her yet?"

Brian shook his head and thought of the senator just down the hall. "No, I imagine she went to see her *fiancé* first." He tried to keep the bitterness out of his voice, but it hurt to say those words. Especially knowing who the fiancé was.

Alex's face crumpled in confusion. "Fiancé?"

"Senator Black," Brian answered simply.

Alex's eyes went wide with surprise. "I have no idea where you heard that, but I can safely say there is no way in h—" He stopped and looked at Grace. "Sorry. Trust me, Brian, there's no way she's engaged to that man." Disgust tinged his words.

"I..." Confused, Brian took a step back. "I read about it in the *Nashville Daily* a few days ago."

Alex shook his head. "No. After what he did, there is no way."

Brian felt the vice cinched around his heart for the past several days loosen. Krisi wasn't engaged to be married to the senator. His breath came easier.

And his curiosity was piqued. What had the senator done to provoke that reaction from Krisi's brother?

Brian was the fifth of twelve bachelors to be auctioned that evening. He'd spent the last hour with Alex, listening to everything that transpired at their family dinner. It took all his self-restraint not to go straight back to the greenroom and pummel Senator Black. He was extraordinarily proud to hear how Krisi had handled herself. Thinking back to seeing Senator Black earlier, he realized the man's nose *had* looked a little swollen. He must have been wearing makeup since his eyes didn't appear bruised. He wondered why she hadn't pressed charges. Even more, he wondered when he was going to see her again.

There were still pieces of the puzzle that didn't make sense. Namely, the text message confirming the engagement. And who wrote the newspaper article? And where did they get the information?

A hand on his shoulder jolted him out of his thoughts. "Mr. Streatt, time to get ready. You're next." One of the event volunteers led him to the wings to wait for Grace to finish the bidding on the bachelor before him. "It'll be just a couple of minutes, then Grace will introduce you and you can go out."

The woman walked away, and Brian stood watching the bids for the man ahead of him.

"I wonder if Grace will even get the minimum five-hundred-dollar-bid for you."

Brian didn't have to turn around to know Senator Black was behind him. He could feel his blood pressure rise, and his hands balled into fists.

The senator scoffed. "A *doorman*."

He stood a few feet behind Brian, who was now tense and frustrated.

"Ladies and gentlemen," Grace said smoothly, "please welcome local businessman Brian Streatt, our next bachelor."

She waited while Brian walked out and sat next to her. He took a deep breath and focused on Grace, getting the senator's comments and energy out of his head.

"If you've been to The Athenian, *the* premiere luxury apartment building downtown, you've probably met Brian. That's where I met him, and I'm grateful to count him as a friend." She smiled, setting him at ease. "Brian not only owns the building, he owns several rental apartments inside it and the retail space on the first floor."

Brian glanced in the wings to where Senator Black was still standing. It may have been petty, but Brian took pleasure in the dumbfounded look on the senator's face. He turned back to Grace and grinned. Now he could relax and enjoy the evening.

"Brian has set up a wonderful date for us. The lucky winner will go on an unforgettable hot air balloon ride to take in views of Nashville and the surrounding countryside at sunrise. After landing, they'll be whisked away to a rooftop champagne breakfast at The Athenian. This date is perfect for both the adventurous and the romantic. We'll start our bidding at five hundred dollars."

The bids were fast and furious for the first several minutes. Brian let out a sigh of relief as the amount went from five hundred to five thousand. He looked around the ballroom at the crowd of mostly women. He wasn't comfortable being the center of attention, but Grace kept it light and fun, which helped his nerves.

Initially, there were several women bidding on his date. Brian recognized one from The Athenian, an elderly woman, one of his long-time residents. He smiled his appreciation at her. When the bidding slowed down, there were only two bidders left—the resident and a young blond woman in the back. Selfishly, he hoped the older woman won, just so he'd know his date. The two bid back and forth until it finally ended at a very respectable twenty-five thousand dollars. The young woman won, and Brian was curious about who she was and why she'd just paid twenty-five thousand to go in a balloon with him.

A volunteer met him offstage and walked him to the payment table, where he met the winning bidder. She introduced herself as Lily and chatted nonstop while paying her bill. Brian grinned at the young woman; she reminded him of Shelby. They were about the same age and had the same outgoing personality. He wondered briefly if he should bring Shelby on the date but realized it would be weird. He could handle one morning with a young woman.

They arranged to meet Saturday at the field where the balloon ride would start. He'd never been in a hot air balloon and was looking forward to it.

Chapter 19

KRISI

KRISI WALKED INTO THE ballroom and slipped into an empty chair at the back to watch the rest of the auction. She was disappointed to have missed Brian, but it couldn't be helped. Her conversation with her father had been longer than expected. And it had been worth the time. She and her father had mended some fences that had been a little battered recently.

She'd then rushed back to her apartment and changed for the auction. She chose a bright pink pantsuit with a lavender silk shell underneath. It was bright and helped keep her mood up while she waited to talk to Brian.

She felt her new phone vibrate in her clutch, signaling a text. She pulled it out and read the short message from her sister.

Sis: done

Krisi smiled, sent a thumbs-up emoji, then slid her phone back into her purse as Grace brought out the next bachelor.

"Next, we have none other than Alexander St. Claire." Krisi looked up as Grace introduced her brother, grinning as he stepped onto the stage. He looked handsome in a royal blue suit, pale pink shirt, and blue suede shoes. His eyes were a shade lighter than his suit. She heard the tittering of women's voices as he sat down next to Grace.

Her brother caused a stir wherever he went. He was oblivious to his impact on the women around him, though. Even Nikki wasn't immune to his charms. She'd had a crush on Alex for years, although living in Europe seemed to have finally cured her of it.

Grace described the date Alex had arranged—a private cooking lesson featuring Southern cuisine with a local chef. In the class, they would learn how to prepare classic dishes, like Nashville hot chicken and shrimp and grits. At the end of the lesson, they would enjoy a candlelit dinner accompanied by a selection of Tennessee wines.

She watched the bidding, humored to see her brother squirm under the attention. He seemed flummoxed when the bidding wound down at fifty thousand. She caught his eye as he was escorted past her and winked.

Krisi sat up a little straighter as Grace introduced the bachelor following Alex. *Senator Michael Black*.

She watched as the senator made his way to the stage. She enjoyed seeing his nose still looked swollen. Unlike her brother, the senator was obviously comfortable in the spotlight and bantered with Grace as she explained his date.

This was the bachelor she'd come for, but she didn't pay attention to what his date would be. It didn't matter.

The bidding began. Krisi watched and waited. The pace slowed at ten thousand, and Krisi jumped in. She won the auction with thirteen thousand, smirking at how much less it was than her brother's. That had to burn the senator's ego.

Because of where she was sitting, she knew he couldn't see who'd won. She made her way to the table, paid the bill, and left a note for the senator to meet her at seven the following evening at Uncorked.

She didn't want to waste time with him right now. There was someone she wanted to see.

Needed to see.

Krisi rushed back to The Athenian as soon as she got to her car. Stepping through the front doors felt like coming home. How had this place become so woven into her heart? Of course she knew the answer to that.

Brian.

And now her mission was to find him.

His office door was still locked, so she stepped into the elevator and pushed the number two button. The short ride to the second floor wasn't long enough to soothe her skittish nerves. She was excited to see him, but the longer it took to find him, the more anxious she became. Her knock on his apartment door went unanswered.

Dejected, she went back to the elevator and rode it to the sixth floor. Her apartment seemed empty and lonely. Standing in her living room, looking out the large window, Krisi felt disappointed. She wanted to see Brian, and the fact that she couldn't find him left her unsettled.

She went to her bedroom and changed into jeans and a baggy sweater. Still unsure what to do with herself, she poured a glass of wine and flopped down on the couch. Squinting at the setting sun shining in her eyes, she stood again and moved to the window. She was about to lower the blinds when it occurred to her she should watch the sunset from the roof. She'd seen numerous sunrises there, but never a sunset.

Before she could overthink it, she grabbed her wine from the coffee table and the key card Brian had given her to access the roof. In the elevator, she tapped the card and punched the button. The quick ascension of the elevator didn't fully explain the flutters in her stomach. Once on the roof, she walked to the western corner of the building, stopping when she saw Brian, as if he'd been waiting for her.

He'd created a separate sitting area while she was gone, with twinkle lights overhead, a rug under a low coffee table, a couch, and two ottomans. A blanket was draped over the back of the couch.

He turned and grinned at her. "I wondered when you would get here."

As she walked toward him, all the pieces of her heart knit back together. "You could have made it a little easier and left me a note."

"Where's the fun in that?" Rubbing his hands on his jeans, he stood as came she came closer. "Besides, I wasn't sure if you wanted to see me."

He'd been nervous, she realized. Somehow, just knowing that calmed everything in her. She stepped up to him, stopping inches away.

"I know we have a lot to talk about, but right now, I really need to feel your arms around me."

His slow smile warmed her heart. He took the final step and wrapped her in his arms. Every fiber in her body relaxed. She took a deep breath, taking in the scent that was Brian. Her arms wound around his waist, and she lay her head on his chest.

"I missed you," she said.

He kissed the top of her head and pulled her even closer. He held her tightly until their hearts were beating at the same steady pace, then leaned back just enough to look at her.

"You're not engaged to another man, right?"

"Nope." She grinned.

His intense look warmed her all the way to her toes. He leaned down and touched his lips to hers.

Home, she thought. *This is home.*

"Just so you know," he said slowly. "I have a date with another woman."

"What?" Krisi leaned back, her eyes wide.

"Yeah. I was part of Grace's bachelor auction, and I have to go on a balloon ride with a young woman." Krisi relaxed as he explained.

"I don't want to. I'd rather go with you, but I agreed to this months ago. Before I met you."

She tightened her grip around him again. "It's okay, Brian. I trust you."

They spent the evening cuddling on the couch, looking at the stars. Brian told her how his week had gone, thinking she was engaged to the senator. She explained how she'd had no way to get in touch with him since her phone was missing.

"Wait." He looked at her, his eyebrows pulling together. "Your phone is missing?"

"Yes. I haven't had it since the dinner with my parents."

"Then...how did you respond to my text?"

"What? What do you mean?" she asked. "Someone responded to you?"

He pulled up the text thread and showed it to her. Her eyes went wide as she read the message saying she was engaged and needed him to leave her alone. There was only one person who would respond in such a manner...but how had the senator gotten her phone? It had to have been during the tussle at her parents' house. She couldn't figure out how he'd grabbed it from her pocket without anyone seeing, without her noticing.

"Do you have plans tomorrow night?" she asked.

Brian shook his head.

"You do now. May I borrow your phone?"

She sent a short text to her old phone before adding her new number.

Senator Black was going to learn not to mess with Krisi St. Claire.

Chapter 20

MICHAEL

A SMILE CROSSED MICHAEL Black's lips as he read the text on Kristine's phone.

BRIAN: Tonight it really hit me who you are. I'll leave you alone. I hope you get everything you deserve

Finally, he thought, *the doorman knows his rightful place.* It's not with Kristine. Kristine was his, whether she realized it or not. He'd been a little out of control at Robert's house, but it just showed how passionate he was. And she'd responded with passion.

That she hadn't pursued anything with the police indicated she knew her place was with him. That she'd placed the winning bid at the auction and left him a note to meet tomorrow night spoke volumes.

After years of planning, everything was coming together. His revenge was almost complete.

"You know this won't bring me back."

Black twirled around to find his mother staring at him. She hadn't come to him in years. She looked like he remembered her—young, healthy. Alive.

"I know it won't, but somebody needs to pay for what they did to you," he said softly.

"You've paid, Michael. You've spent your whole life pursuing vengeance. When will it be over? When will you let me rest in peace?"

He turned from her and stared out at the dark sky. "When the St. Claire family suffers as much as I have."

"Darling." Her soft voice was closer now. "You need to let this go and move on with your life. It will destroy you if you continue."

He turned back to argue his case, but she was gone. He slumped in the leather chair, feeling her loss all over again.

His mother had worked for a small engineering firm that contracted with St. Claire Industries. She'd been one of their best and brightest engineers. George St. Claire, Robert's father, had wined and dined her, trying to get her to work for him. When she declined his offer, he stole her designs. Instead of buying her out, which he could have easily done, he took what he wanted regardless of consequences. He destroyed her and the whole Black family, and in the process, he made billions.

Black had been sixteen when George St. Claire started the campaign to discredit and ruin his mother. St. Claire filed a lawsuit against her when she claimed he'd stolen her designs and spread all kinds of horrible untruths about her. Their solidly middle class family lost everything trying to fight the St. Claire empire.

It had nearly destroyed Michael when he came home from school to find his mother had taken her own life. St. Claire had used it as an admission of guilt, but Michael knew the truth and had sworn revenge against the St. Claire family.

And now, after years of patient planning, it was all coming together.

He understood Kristine wasn't the one who ruined his life, and he almost felt bad about what was coming to her. Heck, it wasn't even her father's fault. Most likely, no living St. Claire knew about their connection. But someone *had* to pay.

His mother hadn't even been worth mentioning when Robert took over. Surely, if he'd known about the sordid connection, he would have had reservations about the two of them working together. But George had died from a heart attack several years earlier, before Black could exact his revenge. So he had no choice but to ruin those who were left.

And Streatt, the unworthy doorman, had just cleared the path for him.

He opened his desk drawer and took out a black velvet box holding the engagement ring he'd bought for this occasion. He couldn't wait to put it on Kristine's lovely finger. With only twenty-four hours until his planning came to fruition, his patience was being tested.

Chapter 21

KRISI

Three wishes:

- *I wish to be brave enough to do what I have to do.*

- *Brave enough to say what I need to say.*

- *And brave enough to share my heart with the man I love.*

THE NEXT EVENING, KRISI sat with Brian at a small table in a corner at Uncorked. Tonight would, hopefully, be the last time she'd have to deal with the senator. She twirled the stem of her wineglass, her nerves tense at what was about to happen. She hadn't spoken to Senator Black since the evening at her parents' house, and after tonight, she wouldn't have to be face-to-face with him again. Except maybe in court.

She stood, kissed Brian lightly on the lips and walked across the bar to a table in another corner. Two men were seated at the table next to her, watching sports on a television above the bar, but otherwise the room was empty. From her seat, she watched the front door, anxiously awaiting Senator Black's arrival.

Two minutes later, the door swung open and Black stepped inside. His gaze locked on Krisi and sent a chill down her spine. He stood frozen for a moment, just staring at her. It was unsettling, but she forced herself to meet his gaze, unflinching. He walked to her slowly, his eyes never leaving hers. She could feel arrogance oozing from him. When he reached her table, he stood for a moment and stared, as if assessing her. Finally, he pulled out the chair opposite her and sat.

"Kristine, it's good to see you." His voice was low and slithered over her. It took all her self-control and training to not shiver at his words.

"Senator," she said without inflection. "I appreciate you meeting me here."

Shelby came over and took his order. She gave Krisi a slight nod that bolstered her courage. She knew the only way to get through the evening was by having people around to watch out for her. And she appreciated them all.

Black took a small black velvet box from his suit pocket and set it on the table between them. She didn't look at it but kept her gaze on him.

"I had intended to give this to you at your father's house, but things ended rather...badly that evening, didn't they?"

Rather badly? Was he serious? For the first time, she looked at the box, then back to him.

Her lack of reaction seemed to test his patience.

He stopped talking when Shelby returned with his drink. With a nod, he dismissed her and refocused on Krisi.

"I've already spoken to your father about this, but now it's time to ask you. Will you marry me, Kristine? You are everything I've ever dreamed about."

She looked at him, incredulous. "You want to *marry* me?"

He let out a sigh. "Yes, darling. I've forgiven you for your impulsive actions the other night."

She carefully unlocked her hands and brought her wine glass closer. She wasn't convinced she could pick it up without her hand shaking, but holding it gave her something to do with her hand.

"And you trying to choke me, what was that? Foreplay?"

His eyes narrowed, and he breathed in sharply. He picked up his scotch and took a generous swig. She watched as he closed his eyes for a moment. When he opened them back up and looked at her, his eyes were emotionless. *Chilling*.

"I didn't want to do that, Kristine, but you left me no choice. I'm grateful the police came to calm you down."

He looked down at the box she still hadn't touched and opened it. Inside sat a gorgeous pear-shaped diamond, probably five carats, on a white gold band.

"I'm willing to overlook what happened and start a new chapter. Together." He slid the case closer to her.

She shook her head at his interpretation of the events at her parents' house. This is one of the reasons she was thankful Alex had the whole interaction on video. Black was *not* going to gaslight her.

"But it was *you* the police took away from the house, not me," she said bluntly.

"Yes." He sighed. "I was grateful for their protection. You were fierce."

"I remember events differently."

"If things happened as you suggest, why didn't you file a police report? Obviously, we need to just move on." He inched the ring closer to her. "Say yes, Kristine. Put my ring on your finger."

She reached into her purse, pulled out some papers, and set them on the table in front of him, then closed the box and slid it back to the center of the table. The papers were a copy of the police report.

As he flipped through the pages, she could see the vein on the side of his neck throb. He looked at her and shook his head. "Kristine, darling. Do you want me to file a police report too? This is ridiculous, and you know it."

He ripped the papers in half and tossed them on the floor.

"You don't mean this any more than I would if I filed a report. Let's move past that whole ugly evening. A fresh start is all we need."

He reopened the ring box and moved it toward her again.

"Senator." She took a deep breath. "Michael, you know I can't marry you. You don't love me any more than I love you."

His eyes narrowed again. "Surely, you know people at our level don't marry for love. We marry for power. *I* have power, Kristine."

"I don't want or need your power, Michael."

She reached out and again closed the velvet box. Before she could return her hand to her lap, he reached out, his fingers circling her wrist.

"You *need* me, Kristine," he said through gritted teeth.

"No. I don't." She twisted her hand, trying to release it from his grasp. Instead, his fingers tightened. "Senator, hurting me again isn't going to make me want to marry you."

He quickly let her go. Picking up the velvet box, he looked at the ring and nodded. "Will you at least try the ring on. Just let me see what it looks like?"

The desperate tone of his voice had the hair on the back of her neck standing on end. She put her hands back in her lap, tightly lacing her fingers, and shook her head.

"I'm sorry, but that's not going to happen."

"Just put the ring on, Kristine."

She watched spittle fly from his mouth and land on her wineglass. She shook her head in disgust but kept her hands locked tight in her lap.

The table shook as his hands slammed down, and he pushed himself to standing.

On the other side of the room, she saw Brian shoot from his chair, but he didn't come forward yet. The senator's chair fell back with a loud clatter, and with shaking fingers, he picked up his scotch and tossed the remaining liquid at her.

Without thinking, she grabbed the napkin off her lap and brought it to her face.

In two steps, Black was in front of her, grabbing her left hand. With his other hand he picked up the ring box. "You *will* wear my ring."

Before he could get the ring out of the box, the men at the next table stood and pushed him down to the table. Within seconds, his hands were behind his back and cuffs were slapped on his wrists.

At the same time, Brian flew across the room in just a few strides. He put his hands on her shoulders and looked her over. "Are you okay?" he asked desperately.

At her nod, he pulled her in for a fierce hug. This was what she needed. This man's arms around her.

It didn't last long enough; there was too much going on.

Brian scowled at Black, whose face and upper body were still flat on the table, one of the undercover officers holding him down. The other officer plucked the ring box off the table with gloved hands, closed the top, and slid it into an evidence bag.

"I wonder why this ring is so important to you, Senator?" he asked. "What will we find when we have it tested?"

Brian and Krisi backed away from the table as the first officer yanked the senator up and marched him out of the room. The second officer stayed behind to finish up with Krisi and Brian.

"I'll pull the SD card from the camera, and we'll write the report from that. If you don't mind coming by the station tomorrow to read it over and sign the paperwork, we can wrap this up."

"Will the video be allowed in court?" Brian asked.

The officer smiled. "You may not have noticed the sign on the door saying the property was under video surveillance, but we have another camera outside the door and have evidence it was there when he entered. We did everything by the book. You two have a good evening." He nodded and made his way out of the room.

When everyone was gone, Brian pulled her back into his arms. "There were so many times I wanted to rush over here to flatten that man,"

Krisi pulled back just enough to look up at him. "I'm glad you didn't give Black any reason to go after you."

"Nothing would have let me ruin your plan. Besides, I already knew you could handle that man. You can handle anything."

He kissed her forehead and pulled her back in close. She could feel his heart hammering in his chest, the rhythm matching her own. She stayed in his embrace until their hearts slowed.

"Brian," she said against his chest, "I love that you trust me."

He tilted his head down, an odd expression on his face. Neither of them had used the word *love*. And while she hadn't said *I love you*, she liked the feel of the word on her lips.

"Of course I trust you. You are one of the bravest and smartest women I know. I trust you with everything." He leaned down and briefly touched his lips to hers.

"Everything?" She smiled up at him. "Even your heart?" She watched carefully as his expression changed from confusion to surprise. She waited for a smile, but it didn't come.

"My heart? You've had that from the beginning, Krisi. Didn't you know that?"

*This...*she thought, *this is what bliss feels like.*

Chapter 22

BRIAN

S ATURDAY MORNING, AT THE crack of dawn, Brian parked in a field outside Nashville. It was still dark, but up ahead, he could see the inflated balloon pulling its tethers. He made his way across the field, ready to fulfill his obligation. His date—Lily—didn't appear to have arrived yet. They'd communicated via text a couple of times, and he double-checked to make sure this was the right day and time.

He walked to the balloon and introduced himself to the men setting it up. Then he stood back and watched as they finished inflating the huge balloon. He felt his phone vibrate in his pocket.

LILY: almost there

He looked up from his phone to see headlights moving across the field, coming closer and closer. Not for the first time, he wished it was Krisi going up with him. Maybe he'd be able to schedule a balloon ride with her another time.

They hadn't had an opportunity to watch the sunrise together since she got back. Krisi had been busy with the cops the last couple of days, so they hadn't seen much of each other. And he knew jet lag still had her catching up on sleep. He missed those quiet early mornings with her.

The car stopped next to his, and he watched a blond woman get out of the passenger seat. As soon as she was clear, the car pulled away and headed back to the road. It looked like they would be riding together to the breakfast part of the date.

He raised his hand in greeting, and the woman walked toward him in the dark. As if his wish had come true, he watched the

woman morph into Krisi. As soon as he recognized her, he rushed forward and wrapped
his arms around her, pulling her close.

"But...what are you doing here?"

She smiled. "Hopefully, taking a sunrise
balloon ride with the man I love."

His heart stuttered at her words.

This was the first time she'd said she loved
him. Honestly, it was the first time in a long
time someone who wasn't family had said it
to him. He pulled her tighter.

"I love you too." He savored the moment,
but he still didn't understand what she was
doing there. "Someone else bought this experience, right?"

She pulled back just enough to smile up
at him. "I knew I was probably going to be
late to the auction, so I asked Lily, my sister,
to bid for me." She grinned slyly. "You didn't
notice her last name was St. Claire?"

Sheepishly, he shook his head. "I didn't
even look at the paperwork. She introduced
herself as Lily, and that was that. I can't tell you
how pleased I am to be going up with you this

morning instead of her...nothing against Lily, of course."

"Of course."

Krisi unwound her arms from his waist and slid them up his chest, leaving a tingling path of warmth in their wake, then wound them around his neck.

"Lily went into this with her eyes wide open." She grinned. "Now tell me you love me again. I kinda liked hearing it."

"Ms. St. Claire." He looked deep into her blue eyes, seeing the love she had for him reflected there. "I love you more than I know what to do with." He lowered his head, and his lips touched hers lightly.

She pulled his head down to hers, stopping a breath from his lips. "I can give you some ideas if you need them." She gave him a light tug and planted her lips on his.

He poured all the feelings he didn't know what to do with into this kiss, hoping she could feel what he didn't know how to express.

"Ahem."

Brian pulled away and looked over his shoulder.

"Sorry to interrupt you," the balloon pilot said. "We're ready whenever you are."

Brian stepped back but kept one arm around Krisi. "Thank you. We'll be right there."

Krisi stretched up and brushed her lips to his cheek. "Let's go watch an amazing sunrise together."

They walked arm in arm to the now fully inflated balloon. Early morning fog hugged the ground, covering the balloon's basket. Spotlights, aimed upward, filtered through the fog to create an almost otherworldly scene in front of them.

The pilot introduced himself as Jeff, and they all climbed into the woven wicker basket. The basket felt rugged and sturdy under Brian's hand as he gripped the edge. As soon as he was in, he turned to offer a hand to Krisi. Jeff steered them to one side of the basket while he stood on the other as the balloon was untethered. They slowly rose, just as the first haze of light began changing the landscape below them.

Looking up, Brian saw the colossal balloon billowing overhead, a kaleidoscope of colors lit up from the burner controlling their ascent. The quiet morning was intermittently interrupted by the roar of the burner overhead.

They stood at the edge of the basket, looking down at the shrinking field. Behind them, a small wooden table, secured to the base, held a picnic hamper. Once they were at cruising height, Jeff nodded toward it. "Help yourselves to something to eat or drink, if you'd like."

Brian nodded, but the scene in front of them captured their attention. They stood, arms wrapped around each other, watching the show. The sunrise from this height was stunning. Mother Nature cooperated by offering a clear sky and showing off all her colors. The sky morphed from pale yellow to deep orange, red, and even a little purple this morning.

Once the sun was fully above the horizon, Krisi turned to face him and touched her lips to his. "This is incredible."

He would have liked to have kept her in his embrace longer to extend the kiss, but having an audience wasn't ideal. She grinned, seeming to understand what was going through his mind.

"I'll see what goodies are in the basket." Her eyes twinkled as she turned to the table. His lips still tingled where her lips had touched.

Within a couple of minutes, Krisi handed him a long, slim champagne flute. "A bellini," she said with a smile. "Since we haven't eaten anything, I was kinda wimpy with the champagne."

He grinned at her and touched his glass to hers. "I don't need champagne. You're all I need to make my head and my heart buzz."

"I'm not sure how I got lucky enough to capture your heart, Brian Streatt." She looked intently at him. "And just so you know, you've had mine all along too."

He carefully set their glasses on the table so he could wrap both arms around her again. He needed her close, so he gathered her in and held her tight until their hearts beat at the same pace.

"Is it any wonder I'm in love with you?" he asked, staring into her mesmerizing eyes. "You're smart, adventurous, creative, fun...oh, and gorgeous."

"What would you think," she started, then took a big breath and let it out slowly. "What would you think about letting me hold your heart for the rest of our lives?"

He felt his eyes go wide. He could see she was nervous. She chewed her lower lip as she waited for his response.

"Are you asking me to marry you?"

She nodded, her eyes cloudy with concern. "Yeah, I guess I am."

He laughed and pulled her in close. "I was going to ask you tonight. I have a ring waiting for you in my apartment."

Then he pulled back to see her eyes had gone wide and a smile was now on her lips.

"To answer your question, yes. I will happily marry you."

Epilogue

KRISI

Three wishes:

- *I have everything I could possibly want!*

Krisi paced the length of the lobby, nerves getting the best of her. Tonight, Brian was meeting her family. Well, he'd already met Alex and Lily, so he was meeting her parents. She walked back into the lobby and plopped onto a chair by the front windows. She looked down at the ring on her left hand. She'd had it for a week and still wasn't used to seeing it there. Brian had given her the perfect engagement ring, and it was stunning.

When they'd gotten back from the balloon ride, he'd dashed to his apartment before meeting her on the roof for their champagne breakfast. Melody had helped him pull off the breakfast. When they stepped onto the roof, it had taken her breath away. There were flowers everywhere—pale pink roses, her favorite.

Before they sat down at the table for the delicious meal awaiting them, Brian dropped down to one knee and held out a Tiffany blue ring box. The ring, now on her third finger, was unlike anything she'd seen before. A pink round-cut diamond was set on a platinum band with nine small round diamonds running along each side. But what made it special were the sixteen small marquise-cut diamonds, leaves of a vine draping the center stone. To say that Brian had chosen the perfect ring for her was an understatement.

The elevator doors opened, and Brian stepped through. He took her breath away with how handsome he was. She stood and smiled as he walked to her. Under his black suit jacket, he wore a vest she'd brought back from Paris.

"You look quite handsome, Mr. Streatt." She put her hand on his chest.

He grinned at her. "It must be my new vest." He tugged the bottom of the pink-and-black double-breasted vest. "Is this okay to wear to dinner?"

She realized he was as nervous as she was. It was, after all, a big deal to bring him to meet her parents. If dinner weren't a formal occasion, she'd prefer to ride over on his motorcycle. He wrapped his arms around her and brought her close. Her nerves dissolved in his arms.

"You look perfect," she said. "I can't tell you not to be nervous, but I will tell you, tonight will be just fine."

She had no idea what her parents would think of Brian, but honestly, she didn't care. He was everything *she* wanted.

They took her car, and he held her hand throughout the trip, rubbing his thumb across her knuckles. All too soon, they arrived and parked behind Alex's black SUV.

They stepped out of the car and stood looking up at the imposing house. She reached over and put her arm around his waist, pulling him close.

"I love you," she said.

He looked down and smiled at her. "I love you too."

She nodded. "Let's do this."

They walked up the steps, and the front door opened before them. Harold nodded. "Miss Kristine."

"Harold," she greeted him. "I'd like you to meet my fiancé, Brian Streatt. Brian, this is Harold. He does a brilliant job keeping the house in tip-top shape and running like a dream."

A small smile escaped Harold's lips before he returned to his solemn expression. He nodded at Brian. "A pleasure to meet you, Mr. Streatt. Follow me to the terrace."

Krisi raised an eye at Brian and mouthed *The terrace?* Why weren't they eating in the dining room? They followed Harold through the house to the back terrace, where the family waited. Twinkle lights sparkled in the trees, lending a festive atmosphere to the evening.

"Kristine." Her father greeted her warmly as soon as they stepped through the doors. He gave her a hug, then turned to Brian. "Robert St. Claire, it's a pleasure to meet the man who captured Kristine's heart."

"Brian Streatt." Brian shook his hand. "A pleasure to meet you, sir."

"Please, call me Robert. We are, after all, going to be family."

Krisi felt some of the tension leave her body. Her father was accepting Brian without hesitation.

Alex came over and shook Brian's hand. "Hey, Brian. It's great to see you again. Congratulations!"

Lily came over next and hugged Brian. "Good to see you again, Brian. I hope you don't mind the subterfuge at the auction...I think you still owe me a balloon ride."

Brian laughed. "You got it."

Krisi grabbed his hand and walked to her mother, who'd been quietly watching. "Mother, I'd like you to meet Brian."

Brian shook her hand. "It's a pleasure to meet you, Mrs. St. Claire. You have a beautiful home. Thank you for letting me join you tonight."

Krisi watched her mother as her mother watched Brian. They stood quietly for several awkward seconds before her mother spoke. "Krisi, may I borrow Brian for a minute?"

Krisi could feel her eyes go wide. Why in the world did her mother want to talk to Brian? Alone? "Of course, Mother."

She squeezed Brian's hand and left the two of them to get a glass of wine.

Two hours later, Brian pulled Krisi's car into the underground garage at The Athenian and turned off the engine. "You up for a nightcap?"

"Sure." She liked the idea of stretching out the evening a little longer. "Let's go to Uncorked."

Hand in hand, they walked down the hallway to the wine bar. It was busy, and only two seats were open at the bar.

"Evenin', folks." Beau was behind the bar. "I understand congratulations are in order."

Krisi grinned at him. "Thanks, Beau. How'd you hear the news?"

"Melody is taking credit for getting you two together."

Krisi and Brian laughed.

"And now, she and her sisters think it's their duty to find someone for me." He rolled his eyes. "Anyway, what can I get y'all tonight? Champagne?"

Brian looked at Krisi, then nodded. "Champagne would be perfect."

Beau popped the cork on a chilled bottle, brought it to them, then filled two long-stemmed flutes. He slid the glasses across the bar. "While I'm happy for you two, I'm not thrilled with my prospects. Melody, Faith, and Harmony need a different project."

Krisi laughed. "You got something against love?"

Beau was thoughtful for a minute. "No, not at all. For others. I just don't think it's in the cards for me."

He wandered to the other end of the bar and Krisi turned to Brian. "Cheers, love of my life."

Brian's face lit up with a smile. "Cheers to you, my love."

"So…" Krisi set her glass on the bar. "What did you and my mother talk about?" She'd been dying to ask.

Brian turned his stool to face her. "Evelyn ask—"

"Evelyn?" Krisi interrupted.

Brian laughed. "Your mother said I should call her Evelyn. It's her name, right?"

"It is." Krisi nodded. "Sorry to interrupt. Keep going."

"Okay." He grinned. "Evelyn asked if I loved you and if I saw you as a lifetime partner."

Krisi felt her eyebrows rise. "And?"

"Of course I told her yes, I love you, and yes, I see you as my partner for the rest of my life"

Krisi's heart melted at his words. "Was that it?"

"Well, she gave me these." He reached into his coat pocket, pulled out a small jewelry box, and handed it to Krisi.

Her curiosity piqued, she opened the box. "Oh my gracious!" Tears prickled her eyes.

"What?"

"Did she tell you about these?"

He shook his head.

"They were my grandfather's, her father's, cufflinks" The box held two golden circles with three small diamonds on each cufflink. She rubbed her thumb across one and smiled.

"Wow. That was nice of her."

He still didn't have the whole story. "My grandfather wore suits to work every day, and these were my favorite of his cufflinks. When I was little, he told me they were his lucky cufflinks. Every morning he wore them, he'd rub them and make three wishes. One wish for each diamond. And that was why he was such a successful man, both in love and in business."

Brian looked at her and gently touched the genie's lamp hanging on the chain around her neck.

She nodded. "The grandmother who gave this to me, the cufflinks belonged to her husband. She knew I liked them."

She looked at the cufflinks and rubbed a finger over them again.

"So it looks like you'll get to make your own *three wishes*."

He put his arm around her waist and leaned close. "You've already given me everything I could wish for."

Thanks for reading Brian & Krisi's story!
If you'd like to stay in their world a little bit
longer, I have a Bonus Epilogue for you.
It's at Brian & Krisi's engagement party

See what happens next: https://bit.ly/BB
BonusChapter

(and, just a little FYI...something does!)

I have two favors to ask of you, dear reader.
If you enjoyed this book, and since you've
made it this far I sincerely hope you did, please
share a picture on social media and tag me.
On Instagram I'm @beckilee_author and on
Facebook I'm @Becki Lee, Author
The second favor is to share a short review on
Amazon of why you liked this book. It doesn't
have to be fancy or long, but it makes a big
difference to me.

Leave a review on Amazon

Also by Becki Lee

Nashville Hearts series
Rescuing Hope
Finding Dolly
Dating Breena
Discovering Jillian
Marrying Grace

Nashville Billionaire series
Betting on Brian
Remembering Beau
Always Alex
Taming Xavier

Acknowledgements

There are always so many people to thank by the time I've finished writing a book. My fear is that I'll forget someone. So, if I have I profusely apologize.

Thank you first and foremost to God, who for some reason has given me an over-active imagination and continually supplies me with more story ideas than I'll ever be able to write. I hope I do the ideas you give me justice.

Thank you to you, dear reader! While I'd probably still write without you, you make this journey so much sweeter. I absolutely love hearing your comments about my books and meeting you in person when we get the opportunity. I'll keep writing and I hope you continue to read my books.

The next big thank you is to my writing community. I am utterly gobsmacked, I love that word, by how big my writing community has grown in such a short time. To everyone at Florida Star Fiction Writers who have encouraged me for the past two years, you're the best and I absolutely love you all. To Kerry Evelyn who is such an amazing writer, beta reader, cheerleader, and friend – thank you!! To Leah who keeps my butt in the chair writing with our almost daily sprints – I can't wait until it's your book we're celebrating!

To Elana Johnson, Bonnie Paulson, Jennifer Probst, and all the authors who are way ahead of me in this journey and share their wisdom, I so appreciate you and your knowledge.

And to my family! My husband is the reason I have a hard time writing anything other than cinnamon roll heroes, lol. Thank you for putting up with my crazy ideas and indulging my need to escape now and again.

About the author

B ECKI WRITES SWEET CONTEMPORARY
romance filled with humor, heartwarm-
ing friendships, and leading ladies who know
how to hold their ground on the way to happily ever after.

With a knack for delicious food descriptions
that might make you reach for a snack and
settings so vivid you'll feel like you've booked
a ticket, her stories offer a full sensory experience.

As a wife of 25+ years, a proud empty nester
with two adult children, and a self-proclaimed
travel addict with a backpack always at the

ready, Becki knows a thing or two about adventure—and she's not afraid to write it!

When she's not crafting stories, she's probably planning her next trip or convincing herself that "research" absolutely requires a taste test.